Over.

That is what my life is. O-V-E-R.

I know I have said that before, but this time I really mean it.

And why? Why THIS TIME?

Because I have a boyfriend.

Isn't that great? Sometimes I think I must be the luckiest girl in the whole world. I mean, really. Think about it: I may not be pretty, but I am not grossly disfigured; I live in New York City, the coolest place on the planet; I'm a princess; I have a boyfriend. What more could a girl ask for?

Oh, God.

WHO AM I KIDDING?????

This boyfriend of mine? Here's the scoop:

I DON'T EVEN LIKE HIM.

Books by

MEG CABOT

THE PRINCESS DIARIES

THE PRINCESS DIARIES, VOLUME II:
PRINCESS IN THE SPOTLIGHT

THE PRINCESS DIARIES, VOLUME III:
PRINCESS IN LOVE

THE PRINCESS DIARIES, VOLUME IV:
PRINCESS IN WAITING

PRINCESS LESSONS:
A PRINCESS DIARIES BOOK

ALL-AMERICAN GIRL

HAUNTED: A TALE OF THE MEDIATOR

NICOLA AND THE VISCOUNT

VICTORIA AND THE ROGUE

MEG CABOT

The Princess Diaries, Volume III

Princess in Love

♛ HarperTrophy®
An Imprint of HarperCollinsPublishers

Harper Trophy® is a registered trademark of
HarperCollins Publishers Inc.

Princess in Love
Copyright © 2002 by Meggin Cabot

Library of Congress Cataloging-in-Publication Data
Cabot, Meg.
   Princess in love / Meg Cabot.
     p.   cm. — (The princess diaries ; v. 3)
   Summary: In a series of humorous diary entries, a New York
City ninth grader agonizes over her love life, final exams, and
future role as the princess of Genovia.
   ISBN 0-06-029467-1 — ISBN 0-06-029468-X (lib. bdg.)
   ISBN 0-06-447280-9 (pbk.)
   [1. Princesses—Fiction. 2. Identity—Fiction. 3. Schools—
Fiction. 4. Love—Fiction. 5. New York (NY)—Fiction.
6. Diaries—Fiction. 7. Humorous stories.] I. Title. II. Series.
PZ7.C11165 Ps 2002   2001039815
[Fic]—dc21   CIP
                                                     AC

Typography by Alison Donalty
❖
First Harper Trophy edition, 2002
Visit us on the World Wide Web! www.harperteen.com

For Benjamin, with love

ACKNOWLEDGMENTS

Many thanks to Beth Ader, Jennifer Brown, Barbara Cabot, Sarah Davies, Laura Langlie, Abby McAden, and David Walton.

"One of Sara's 'pretends' is that she is a princess," said Jessie. "She plays it all the time—even in school. She wants Ermengarde to be one, too, but Ermengarde says she is too fat."

"She is too fat," said Lavinia. "And Sara is too thin."

"Sara says it has nothing to do with what you look like, or what you have. It has only to do with what you think of, and what you do," Jessie explained.

A LITTLE PRINCESS
Frances Hodgson Burnett

Assignment (Due December 8): Here at Albert Einstein High School, we have a very diverse student population. Over one hundred and seventy different nations, religions, and ethnic groups are represented by our student body. In the space below, describe the manner in which your family celebrates the uniquely American holiday, Thanksgiving. Please utilize appropriate margins.

MY THANKSGIVING
by Mia Thermopolis

6:45 a.m.—Roused by the sound of my mother vomiting. She is well into her third month of pregnancy now. According to her obstetrician, all the throwing up should stop in the next trimester. I can't wait. I have been marking the days off on my 'N Sync calendar. (I don't really like 'N Sync. At least, not that much. My best friend, Lilly, bought me the calendar as a joke. Except that one guy really is pretty cute.)

7:45 a.m.—Mr. Gianini, my new stepfather, knocks on my door. Only now I am supposed to call him Frank. This is very difficult to remember due to the fact that at school, where he is my first-period Algebra teacher, I am supposed to call him Mr. Gianini. So I just don't call him anything (to his face).

It's time to get up, Mr. Gianini says. We are having Thanksgiving at his parents' house on Long Island. We have to leave now if we are going to beat the traffic.

8:45 a.m.–There is no traffic this early on Thanksgiving Day. We arrive at Mr. G's parents' house in Sagaponic three hours early.

Mrs. Gianini (Mr. Gianini's mother, not my mother. My mother is still Helen Thermopolis because she is a fairly well known modern painter under that name, and also because she does not believe in the cult of the patriarchy) is still in curlers. She looks very surprised. This might not only be because we arrived so early, but also because no sooner had my mother entered the house than she was forced to run for the bathroom with her hand pressed over her mouth, on account of the smell of the roasting turkey. I am hoping this means that my future half-brother or -sister is a vegetarian, since the smell of meat cooking used to make my mother hungry, not nauseated.

My mother had already informed me in the car on the way over from Manhattan that Mr. Gianini's parents are very old-fashioned and are used to enjoying a conventional Thanksgiving meal. She does not think they will appreciate hearing my traditional Thanksgiving speech about how the Pilgrims are guilty of committing mass genocide by giving their new Native American friends blankets filled with the smallpox virus, and that it is reprehensible that we as a country annually celebrate this rape and destruction of an entire culture.

Instead, my mother said, I should discuss more neutral topics, such as the weather.

I asked if it was all right if I discussed the astonishingly high rate of attendance at the Reykjavik opera house in Iceland (over 98 percent of the country's population has seen *Tosca* at least once).

My mother sighed and said, "If you must," which I take to be a sign that she is beginning to tire of hearing about Iceland.

Well, I am sorry, but I find Iceland extremely fascinating, and I will not rest until I have visited the ice hotel.

9:45 a.m.–11:45 a.m.–I watch the Macy's Thanksgiving Day parade with Mr. Gianini Senior in what he calls the rec room.

They don't have rec rooms in Manhattan.

Just lobbies.

Remembering my mother's warning, I refrain from repeating another one of my traditional holiday rants, that the Macy's Thanksgiving Day parade is a gross example of American capitalism run amok.

At one point during the broadcast, I catch sight of Lilly standing in the crowd outside of Office Max on Broadway and Thirty-Seventh, her videocamera clutched to her slightly squished-in face (so much like a pug) as a float carrying Miss America and William Shatner of *Star Trek* fame passes by. So I know Lilly is going to take care of denouncing Macy's on the next episode of her public access television show, *Lilly Tells It Like It Is* (every Friday night at nine, Manhattan cable channel 67).

12:00 p.m.—Mr. Gianini Junior's sister arrives with her husband, their two kids, and the pumpkin pies. The kids, who are my age, are twins, a boy, Nathan, and a girl, Claire. I know right away Claire and I are not going to get along, because when we are introduced she looks me up and down the way the cheerleaders do in the hallway at school and goes, in a very snotty voice, "*You're* the one who's supposed to be a princess?"

And while I am perfectly aware that at five foot nine inches tall, with no visible breasts, feet the size of snowshoes, and hair that sits in a tuft on my head like the cotton on the end of a Q-tip, I am the biggest freak in the freshman class of Albert Einstein High School for Boys (made coeducational circa 1975), I do not appreciate being reminded of it by girls who do not even bother finding out that beneath this mutant facade beats the heart of a person who is only striving, just like everybody else in this world, to find self-actualization.

Not that I even care what Mr. Gianini's niece

Claire thinks of me. I mean, she is wearing a pony-skin miniskirt. And it is not even imitation pony skin. She must know that a horse had to die just so she could have that skirt, but she obviously doesn't care.

Now Claire has pulled out her cell phone and gone out onto the deck, where the reception is best (even though it is thirty degrees outside, she apparently doesn't mind. She has that pony skin to keep her warm, after all). She keeps looking in at me through the sliding glass doors and laughing as she talks on her phone.

Nathan—who is dressed in baggy jeans and has a pager, in addition to a lot of gold jewelry—asks his grandfather if he can change the channel. So instead of traditional Thanksgiving viewing options, such as football or the Lifetime Channel's made-for-TV movie marathon, we are now forced to watch MTV2. Nathan knows all the songs and sings along with them. Most of them have dirty words that have been bleeped out, but Nathan sings them anyway.

1:00 p.m.—The food is served. We begin eating.

1:15 p.m.—We finish eating.

1:20 p.m.—I help Mrs. Gianini clean up. She says not to be ridiculous, and that I should go "have a nice gossip" with Claire.

It is frightening, if you think about it, how clueless old people can be sometimes.

Instead of going to have a nice gossip with Claire, I stay where I am and tell Mrs. Gianini how much I am enjoying having her son live with us. Mr. G is very good about helping around the house, and has even taken over my old job of cleaning the toilets. Not to mention the thirty-six-inch TV, pinball machine, and foozball table he brought with him when he moved in.

Mrs. Gianini is immensely gratified to hear this, you can just tell. Old people like to hear nice stuff about their kids, even if their kid, like Mr. Gianini, is thirty-nine and a half years old.

3:00 p.m.—We have to leave if we are going to beat the traffic home. I say good-bye. Claire does not say good-bye back to me, but Nathan does. He advises me to keep it real. Mrs. Gianini gives us a lot of left-over turkey. I thank her, even though I don't eat turkey, being a vegetarian.

6:30 p.m.—We finally make it back into the city, after spending three and a half hours in bumper-to-bumper traffic along the Long Island Expressway. Though there is nothing very express about it, if you ask me.

I barely have time to change into my baby-blue floor-length Armani sheath dress and matching ballet flats before the limo honks downstairs, and Lars, my bodyguard, arrives to escort me to my second Thanksgiving dinner.

7:30 p.m.–Arrive at the Plaza Hotel. I am greeted by the concierge, who announces me to the masses assembled in the Palm Court:

"Presenting Her Royal Highness Princess Amelia Mignonette Grimaldi Thermopolis Renaldo."

God forbid he should just say Mia.

My father, the prince of Genovia, and his mother, the dowager princess, have rented the Palm Court for the evening in order to throw a Thanksgiving banquet for all of their friends. Despite my strenuous objections, Dad and Grandmère refuse to leave New York City until I have learned everything there is to know about being a princess . . . or until my formal introduction to the Genovian people the day before Christmas, whichever comes first. I have assured them that it isn't as if I am going to show up at the castle and start hurling olives at the ladies-in-waiting and scratching myself under the arms. I mean, I am fourteen years old: I do have some idea how to act, for crying out loud.

But Grandmère, at least, does not seem to believe this, and so she is still subjecting me to daily princess lessons. Lilly recently contacted the United Nations to see whether these lessons constitute a human rights violation. She believes it is unlawful to force a minor to sit for hours practicing tipping her soup bowl away from her—"Always, always, *away* from you, Amelia!"—in order to scrape up a few drops of lobster bisque. The UN has so far been unsympathetic to my plight.

It was Grandmère's idea to have what she calls an "old-fashioned" Thanksgiving dinner, featuring mussels in a white wine sauce, squab stuffed with fois gras, lobster tails, and Iranian caviar, which you could never get before because of the embargo. She has invited two hundred of her closest friends, plus the emperor of Japan and his wife, since they were in town anyway for a world trade summit.

That's why I have to wear ballet flats. Grandmère says it's rude to be taller than an emperor.

8:00 p.m.–11:00 p.m.–I make polite conversation with the empress while we eat. Like me, she was just a normal person until one day she married the emperor and became royal. I, of course, was born royal. I just didn't know it until September, when my dad found out he couldn't have any more kids, due to his chemotherapy for testicular cancer having rendered him sterile. Then he had to admit he was actually a prince and all, and that though I am "illegitimate," since my dad and my mom were never married, I am still the sole heir to the Genovian throne.

And even though Genovia is a very small country (population 50,000) crammed into a hillside along the Mediterranean Sea between Italy and France, it is still this very big deal to be princess of it.

Not a big enough deal for anyone to raise my allowance higher than ten dollars a week, apparently. But a big enough deal that I have to have a bodyguard follow me around everywhere I go, just in case some Euro-trash terrorist in a ponytail and black leather pants takes it into his head to kidnap me.

The empress knows all about this—what a bummer it is, I mean, being just a normal person one day, and then having your face on the cover of *People* magazine the next. She even gave me some advice: She told me I should always make sure my kimono is securely fastened before I raise my arm to wave to the populace.

I thanked her, even though I don't actually own a kimono.

11:30 p.m.—I am so tired on account of having gotten up so early to go to Long Island, I have yawned in the empress's face twice. I have tried to hide these yawns the way Grandmère taught me to, by clenching my jaw and refusing to open my mouth. But this only makes my eyes water, and the rest of my face stretch out like I am hurtling through a black hole. Grandmère gives me the evil eye over her salad with pears and walnuts, but it is no use. Even her malevolent stare cannot shake me from my state of extreme drowsiness.

Finally, my father notices, and grants me a royal

reprieve from dessert. Lars drives me back to the apartment. Grandmère is clearly upset because I am leaving before the cheese course. But it is either that, or pass out in the *fromage bleu*. I know that in the end, Grandmère will have retribution, undoubtedly in the form of forcing me to learn the names of every member of the Swedish royal family, or something equally as heinous.

Grandmère always gets her way.

12:00 a.m.—After a long and exhausting day of giving thanks to the founders of our nation—those genocidal hypocrites known as the Pilgrims—I finally go to bed.

And that concludes Mia Thermopolis's Thanksgiving.

Saturday, December 6

Over.

That is what my life is. O-V-E-R.

I know I have said that before, but this time I really mean it.

And why? Why THIS TIME? Surprisingly, it's not because:

Three months ago, I found out that I'm the heir to the throne of a small European nation, and that at the end of this month, I am going to have to go to said small European nation and be formally introduced for the first time to the people over whom I will one day reign, and who will undoubtedly hate me, because given that my favorite shoes are my combat boots and my favorite TV show is *Baywatch*, I am so not the royal-princess type.

Or because:

My mother, who is expecting to give birth to my Algebra teacher's child in approximately seven months, recently eloped with said Algebra teacher.

Or even because:

At school they've been loading us down with so much homework—and after school, Grandmère's been torturing me so endlessly with all the princess stuff I've got to learn by Christmas—that I haven't even been able to keep up with this journal, let alone anything else.

Oh, no. It's not because of any of that. Why is my life over?

Because I have a boyfriend.

At fourteen years of age, I suppose it's about time. I mean, all my friends have boyfriends. All of them, even Lilly, who blames the male gender for most, if not all, of society's ills.

And okay, Lilly's boyfriend is Boris Pelkowski, who may, at the age of fifteen, be one of the nation's leading violin virtuosos, but that doesn't mean he doesn't tuck his sweater into his pants, or that he doesn't have food in his braces more often than not. Not what I would call ideal boyfriend material, but Lilly seems to like him, which is all that matters.

I guess.

I have to admit, when Lilly—possibly the pickiest person on this planet (and I should know, having been best friends with her since kindergarten)—got a boyfriend, and I still didn't have one, I pretty much started to think there was something wrong with me. Besides my gigantism and what Lilly's parents, the Drs. Moscovitz, who are psychiatrists, call my inability to verbalize my inner rage.

And then, one day, out of the blue, I got one. A boyfriend, I mean.

Well, okay, not out of the blue. Kenny started sending me all these anonymous love letters. I didn't know it was him. I kind of thought (okay, hoped) someone else was sending them. But in the end, it turned out to be Kenny. And by then I was in too deep, really, to get out. So *voila*! I had a boyfriend.

Problem solved, right?

Not. So not.

And it isn't that I don't like Kenny. I do. I really do. We have a lot in common. For instance, we both appreciate the preciousness of not just human, but *all* life forms, and refuse to dissect fetal pigs and frogs in Bio. Instead, we are writing term papers on the life cycles of various grubs and mealworms.

And we both like science fiction. Kenny knows a lot more about it than I do, but he has been very impressed so far by the extent of my familiarity with the works of Robert A. Heinlein and Isaac Asimov, both of whom we were forced to read in school (though he doesn't seem to remember this).

I haven't told Kenny that I actually find most science fiction boring, since there seem to be very few girls in it.

There are a lot of girl characters in Japanese anime, which Kenny also really likes, and which he has decided to devote his life to promoting (when he is not busy finding a cure for cancer). I have noticed that most of the girls in Japanese anime seem to have misplaced their bras.

Plus I really think it might be detrimental to a fighter pilot to have a lot of long hair floating around in the cockpit while she is gunning down the forces of evil.

But like I said, I haven't mentioned any of this to Kenny. And mostly, we get along great. We have a fun time together. And in some ways, it's very nice to have a boyfriend. Like, I don't have to worry now about not being asked to the Albert Einstein High School Nondenominational Winter Dance (so called because its former title, the Albert Einstein High School Christmas Dance, offended many of our non–Christmas-celebrating students).

And why is it that I do not have to worry about not being asked to the biggest dance of the school year, with the exception of the prom?

Because I'm going with Kenny.

Well, okay, he hasn't exactly asked me yet, but he will. Because he is my boyfriend.

Isn't that great? Sometimes I think I must be the luckiest girl in the whole world. I mean, really. Think about it: I may not be pretty, but I am not grossly disfigured; I live in New York City, the coolest place on the planet; I'm a princess; I have a boyfriend. What more could a girl ask for?

Oh, God.

WHO AM I KIDDING?????

This boyfriend of mine? Here's the scoop:

I DON'T EVEN LIKE HIM.

Well, okay, it's not that I don't like him. But this boyfriend thing, I just don't know. Kenny's a nice enough guy and all—don't get me wrong. I mean, he is funny and not boring to be with, certainly. And he's pretty cute, you know, in a tall, skinny sort of way.

It's just that when I see Kenny walking down the hall, my heart so totally doesn't start beating faster, the way girls' hearts start beating faster in those teen romances my friend Tina Hakim Baba is always reading.

And when Kenny takes my hand, at the movies or whatever, it's not like my hand gets all tingly in his, the way girls' hands do in those books.

And when he kisses me? Those fireworks people always talk about? Forget about it. No fireworks. Nil. Nada.

It's funny, because before I got a boyfriend, I used to spend a lot of time trying to figure out how to get one, and once I got him, how I'd get him to kiss me.

But now that I actually have a boyfriend, mostly all I do is try to figure out how to get out of kissing him.

One way that I have found that works quite effectively is the head turn. If I notice his lips coming toward me, I just turn my head at the last minute, so all he gets is my cheek, and maybe some hair.

I guess the worst thing is, when Kenny gazes deeply into my eyes—which he does a lot—and asks me what I am thinking about, I am usually thinking about this one certain person.

And that person isn't Kenny. It isn't Kenny at all. It is Lilly's older brother, Michael Moscovitz, whom I have loved for, oh, I don't know, MY ENTIRE LIFE.

Wait, though. It gets worse.

Because now it's like everybody considers me and Kenny this big Item. You know? Now we're Kenny-and-Mia. Now, instead of Lilly and me hanging out together Saturday nights, it's Lilly-and-Boris and Kenny-and-Mia. Sometimes my friend Tina Hakim Baba and her boyfriend, Dave Farouq El-Abar, and my other friend Shameeka Taylor and her boyfriend, Daryl Gardner, join us, making it Lilly-and-Boris and Kenny-and-Mia and Tina-and-Dave and Shameeka-and-Daryl.

So if Kenny and I break up, who am I going to hang around with on Saturday nights? I mean, seriously. Lilly-and-Boris and Tina-and-Dave and Shameeka-and-Daryl won't want just plain Mia along. I'll be just like this seventh wheel.

Not to mention, if Kenny and I break up, who will I go to the Nondenominational Winter Dance with? I mean, if he ever gets around to asking me.

Oh, God, I have to go now. Lilly-and-Boris and Tina-and-Dave and Kenny-and-Mia are supposed to go ice-skating at Rockefeller Center.

All I can say is, be careful what you wish for. It just might come true.

Saturday, December 6, 11 p.m.

I thought my life was over because I have a boyfriend now and I don't really like him in that way, and I have to break up with him without hurting his feelings, which is, I guess, probably impossible.

Yeah, well, I didn't know *how* over my life could actually be.

Not until tonight, anyway.

Tonight, Lilly-and-Boris and Tina-and-Dave and Mia-and-Kenny were joined by a new couple, Michael-and-Judith.

That's right: Lilly's brother Michael showed up at the ice-skating rink, and he brought with him the president of the Computer Club—of which he is treasurer—Judith Gershner.

Judith Gershner, like Lilly's brother Michael, is a senior at Albert Einstein High School.

Judith Gershner, like Michael, is on the honor roll.

Judith Gershner, like Michael, will probably get into every college she applies to, because Judith Gershner, like Michael, is brilliant.

In fact, Judith Gershner, like Michael, won a prize last year at the Albert Einstein High School Annual Biomedical Technology Fair for her science project, in which she actually cloned a fruit fly.

She cloned a fruit fly. At home. In her *bedroom*.

Judith Gershner knows how to clone fruit flies in

her bedroom. And me? I can't even multiply fractions.

Hmmm. Gee, I don't know. If you were Michael Moscovitz—you know, a straight-A student who got into Columbia, early decision—who would you rather go out with? A girl who can clone fruit flies in her bedroom, or a girl who is getting a D in Freshman Algebra, in spite of the fact that *her mother is married to her Algebra teacher*?

Not that there's even a chance of Michael ever asking me out. I mean, I have to admit, there were a couple of times when I thought he might. But that was clearly just wishful thinking on my part. I mean, why would a guy like Michael, who does really well in school and will probably excel at whatever career he ultimately chooses, ever ask out a girl like me, who would have flunked out of the ninth grade by now if it hadn't been for all those extra tutoring sessions with Mr. Gianini, and, ironically, Michael himself?

But Michael and Judith Gershner, on the other hand, are perfect for each other. Judith even looks like him, a little. I mean, they both have the same curly black hair and pale skin from being inside all the time, looking up stuff about genomes on the Internet.

But if Michael and Judith Gershner are so suited for each other, how come when I first saw them walking toward us while we were lacing up our rental skates, I got this very bad feeling inside?

I mean, I have absolutely no right to be jealous of

the fact that Michael Moscovitz asked Judith Gershner to go skating with him. Absolutely no right at all.

Except that when I first saw them together, I was shocked. I mean, Michael hardly ever leaves his room, on account of always being at his computer, maintaining his webzine, *Crackhead*. The last place I'd ever expected to see him is the ice-skating rink at Rockefeller Center during the height of the Christmas-tree–lighting hysteria. Michael generally avoids places he considers tourists traps, like pretty much everywhere north of Bleecker Street.

But there he was, and there was Judith Gershner, in her overalls and Rockports and ski parka, chatting away with him about something—probably something really smart, like DNA.

I nudged Lilly in the side—she was lacing up her skates—and said, in this voice that I hoped didn't show what I was feeling inside, "Look, there's your brother."

And Lilly wasn't even surprised to see him! She looked over and saw him and went, "Oh, yeah. He said he might show up."

Show up with a *date*? Did he mention *that*? And would it have been too much for you, Lilly, to have mentioned this to me beforehand, so I could have had time for a little mental preparation?

Only Lilly doesn't know how I feel about her brother, so I guess it never occurred to her to break it to me gently.

Here's the subtle way in which I handled the situation. It was really smooth (NOT).

As Michael and Judith were looking around for a place to put on their skates:

Me: (Casually, to Lilly) I didn't know your
           brother and Judith Gershner were
           going out.
Lilly: (Disgusted for some reason) Please.
           They're not. She was just over at our
           place, working with Michael on some
           project for the stupid Computer Club.
           They heard we were all going skating,
           and Judith said she wanted to come, too.
Me: Well, that sounds like they're going out
           to me.
Lilly: Whatever. Boris, must you constantly
           breathe on me?
Me: (To Michael and Judith as they walk up to
           us) Oh, hi, you guys. Michael, I didn't
           know you knew how to ice-skate.
Michael: (shrugging) I used to be on a hockey
           team.
Lilly: (snorting) Yeah, Pee Wee Hockey. That
           was before he decided that team sports
           were a waste of time because the success of
           the team was dictated by the performance
           of all the players as a whole, as opposed

to sports determined by individual
performance such as tennis and golf.

Michael: Lilly, don't you ever shut up?

Judith: I love ice-skating! Although I'm not very
good at it.

And she certainly isn't. Judith is such a bad skater,
she had to hold on to both of Michael's hands while he
skated backwards in front of her, just to keep from
falling flat on her face. I don't know which astonished
me more: that Michael can skate backwards, or that he
didn't seem to mind having to tow Judith all around the
rink. I mean, I may not be able to clone a fruit fly, but
at least I can remain upright unaided in a pair of ice
skates.

Kenny, however, seemed to really think Michael and
Judith's method of skating was way preferable to skating the old-fashioned way—you know, solo—so he kept
coming up and trying to get me to let him tow me
around the way Michael was towing Judith.

And even though I was all, "Duh, Kenny, I know
how to skate," he said that that wasn't the point.
Finally, after he'd bugged me for like half an hour, I
gave in, and let him hold both my hands as he skated in
front of me, backwards.

Only the thing is, Kenny isn't very good at skating
backwards. I can skate forward, but I'm not good
enough at it that if someone is wobbling around in front

of me, I can keep from crashing into him if he falls down.

Which was exactly what happened. Kenny fell down, and I couldn't stop, so I crashed into him, and my chin hit his knee and I bit my tongue and all this blood filled up my mouth, and I didn't want to swallow it so I spat it out. Only unfortunately it went all over Kenny's jeans and onto the ice, which clearly impressed all of the tourists standing along the railings around the rink, taking pictures of their loved ones in front of the enormous Rockefeller Center Christmas tree, since they all turned around and started taking pictures of the girl spitting up blood on the ice below, a truly New York moment.

And then Lars came *shoosh*ing over—he is a champion ice-skater, thanks to his Nordic upbringing; quite a contrast to his bodyguard training in the heart of the Gobi desert—picked me up, looked at my tongue, gave me his handkerchief and told me to keep pressure on the wound, and then said, "That's enough skating for one night."

And that was it. Now I've got this bloody gouge in the tip of my tongue, and it hurts to talk, and I was totally humiliated in front of millions of tourists who'd come to look at the stupid tree at stupid Rockefeller Center, not to mention in front of my friends and, worst of all, Judith Gershner, who it turns out also got accepted early decision at Columbia (great, the same school Michael's going to in the fall), where she will be pre-med, and who advised me that I should go to the hospital, as it seemed likely to her that I might need stitches. In my *tongue*. I'm lucky, she said, I didn't bite the tip of it off.

Lucky!

Oh, yeah, I'll tell you how lucky I am: I'm so lucky that while I lie here in bed writing this, with no one but my twenty-five-pound cat, Fat Louie, to keep me company (and Fat Louie only likes me because I feed him), the boy I've been in love with since like forever is up at midtown right now with a girl who knows how to clone fruit flies and can tell if wounds need stitches or not.

One good thing about this tongue, though: if Kenny was thinking about moving on to Frenching, we totally can't until I heal. And that could, according to Dr. Fung—whom my mom called as soon as Lars brought me home—take anywhere from three to ten days.

Yes!

TEN THINGS I HATE ABOUT THE HOLIDAY SEASON IN NEW YORK CITY

1. Tourists who come in from out of town in their giant sports utility vehicles and try to run you over at the crosswalks, thinking they are driving like aggressive New Yorkers. Actually, they are driving like morons. Plus there is enough pollution in this city. Why can't they just take public transit, like normal people?
2. Stupid Rockefeller Center tree. They asked me to be the person who throws the switch to light it this year, as I am considered "New York's own Royal" in the press, but when I told them how cutting down trees contributes to the destruction of the ozone layer, they rescinded their invitation and had the mayor do it instead.
3. Stupid Christmas carols blaring from outside all the stores.
4. Stupid ice-skating with stupid boys who think they can skate backwards when they can't.
5. Pressure to buy stupid "meaningful" gifts for everyone you know.
6. Final exams.
7. Stupid lousy New York weather. No snow, just cold, wet rain, every single day. Whatever happened to a white Christmas? I'll tell you:

Global warming. You know why? Because
everybody keeps driving SUVs and cutting
down trees!

8. Stupid manipulative Christmas specials on TV.
9. Stupid manipulative Christmas commercials
on TV.
10. Mistletoe. This stuff should be banned. In
the hands of adolescent boys, it becomes a
societally approved excuse to demand kisses.
This is sexual harassment, if you ask me.

Plus all the wrong boys have it.

Sunday, December 7

Just got back from dinner at Grandmère's. All of my efforts to get out of having to go—even my pointing out that I am currently suffering from a perforated tongue—were in vain.

And this one was even worse than usual. That's because Grandmère wanted to go over my itinerary for my trip to Genovia, which, by the way, looks like this:

Sunday, December 21
3 p.m.
Arrive in Genovia

3:30 p.m.–5 p.m.
Meet and greet palace staff

5 p.m.–7 p.m.
Tour of palace

7 p.m.–8 p.m.
Change for dinner

8 p.m.–11 p.m.
Dinner with Genovian dignitaries

Monday, December 22
8 a.m.–9:30 a.m.
Breakfast with Genovian public officials

10 a.m.–11:30 a.m.
Tour of Genovian public schools

12 p.m.–1 p.m.
Meet with Genovian schoolchildren

1:30 p.m.–3 p.m.
Lunch with members of Genovian Teachers
Association

3:30 p.m.–4:30 p.m.
Tour of Port of Genovia and Genovian naval
cruiser (the *Prince Phillipe*)

5 p.m.–6 p.m.
Tour of Genovian General Hospital

6 p.m.–7 p.m.
Visit with hospital patients

7 p.m.–8 p.m.
Change for dinner

8 p.m.–11 p.m.
Dinner with the dowager princess, prince, and Genovian military advisors

Tuesday, December 23
8 a.m.–9 a.m.
Breakfast with members of Genovian Olive Growers Association

10 a.m.–11 a.m.
Christmas Tree Lighting ceremony, Genovia Palace Courtyard

11:30 a.m.–1 p.m.
Meet with Genovian Historical Society

1 p.m.–3 p.m.
Lunch with Genovian Board of Tourism

3:30 p.m.–5:30 p.m.
Tour of Genovian National Art Museum

6 p.m.–7 p.m.
Visit Genovian War Veterans Memorial, place flowers on grave of Unknown Soldier

7:30 p.m.–8:30 p.m.
Change for dinner

8:30 p.m.–11:30 p.m.
Dinner with Royal Family of Monaco

And so on.

It all culminates in my appearance on my dad's annual nationally televised Christmas Eve address to the people of Genovia, during which he will introduce me to the populace. I am then supposed to make a speech about how thrilled I am to be Dad's heir, and how I promise to try to do as good a job as he has at leading Genovia into the twenty-first century.

Nervous? Me? About going on TV and promising fifty thousand people that I won't let their country down?

Nah. Not me.

I just want to throw up every time I think about it, that's all.

Whatever. Not that I thought my trip to Genovia was going to be like going to Disneyland, but still. You'd think they'd have scheduled in *some* fun time. I'm not even asking for Mr. Toad's Wild Ride. Just, like, some swimming or horseback riding.

But apparently, there is no time for fun in Genovia. As if going over my itinerary wasn't bad enough, I also had to meet my cousin Sebastiano. Sebastiano Grimaldi is my dead grandfather's sister's daughter's kid. Which I guess actually makes him my cousin a couple times removed. But not removed enough that, if it weren't for me, he wouldn't be inheriting the throne to Genovia.

Seriously. If my dad had died without ever having had a kid, Sebastiano would be the next prince of Genovia.

Maybe that's why my dad, every time he looks at Sebastiano, heaves this big shudder.

Or maybe it's just because my dad feels about Sebastiano the way I feel about my cousin Hank: I like him in theory, but in actual practice, he kind of bugs me.

Sebastiano doesn't bug Grandmère, though. You can tell that Grandmère just loves him. Which is really weird, because I always supposed Grandmère was incapable of loving anyone. Well, with the exception of Rommel, her miniature poodle.

But you can tell she totally adores Sebastiano. When she introduced him to me, and he bowed with this big flourish and kissed the air above my hand, Grandmère was practically beaming beneath her pink silk turban. Really.

I have never seen Grandmère beam before. Glare, plenty of times. But never beam.

Which might be why my dad started chewing the ice

in his whiskey and soda in a very irritated manner. Grandmère's smile disappeared right away when she heard all that crunching.

"If you want to chew ice, Phillipe," Grandmère said, coldly, "you can go and have your dinner at McDonald's with the rest of the proletariat."

My dad stopped chewing his ice.

It turns out Grandmère brought Sebastiano over from Genovia so that he could design my dress for my nationally televised introduction to my countrymen. Sebastiano is a very up-and-coming fashion designer— at least according to Grandmère. She says it is important that Genovia supports its artists and craftspeople, or they will all flee to New York, or even worse, Los Angeles.

Which is too bad for Sebastiano, since he looks like the type who might really enjoy living in LA. He is thirtyish, with long, dark hair tied back in a ponytail, and is all tall and flamboyant-looking. Like for instance, tonight, instead of a tie, Sebastiano was wearing a white silk ascot. And he had on a blue velvet jacket with leather pants.

I am fully prepared to forgive Sebastiano for the leather pants if he designs me a dress that is nice enough. A dress that, should he happen to see me in it, will make Michael Moscovitz forget all about Judith Gershner and her fruit flies, and fill his head with nothing but thoughts of me, Mia Thermopolis.

Only of course the chances of Michael ever actually seeing me in this dress are very slim, as my introduction to the Genovian people is only going to be on Genovian television, not CNN or anything.

Still, Sebastiano seemed ready to rise to the challenge. After dinner, he even took out a pen and began sketching—right on the white tablecloth!—a design he thought might accentuate what he called my narrow waist and long legs.

Only, unlike my dad, who was born and raised in Genovia but speaks fluent English, Sebastiano doesn't have a real keen grasp of the language. He kept forgetting the second syllables of words. So *narrow* became "nar." Just like *coffee* became "coff," and when he described something as magical, it came out as "madge." Even the butter wasn't safe. When Sebastiano asked me to please pass him the "butt," I had to practically stuff my napkin in my mouth to keep from laughing out loud.

All my efforts to stifle myself didn't do any good, though, since Grandmère caught me and, raising one of her drawn-on eyebrows, went, "Amelia, kindly do not make light of other people's speech habits. Your own are not even remotely perfect."

Which is certainly true, considering the fact that, with my swollen tongue, I can't really say any word that starts with *s*.

Not only did Grandmère not mind Sebastiano

saying the word *butt* at the dinner table, she didn't mind his drawing on the tablecloth, either. She looked down at his sketch and said, "Brilliant. Simply brilliant. As usual."

Sebastiano looked very pleased. "Do you real think so?" he asked.

Only I didn't think his sketch was so brilliant. It just looked like an ordinary dress to me. Certainly nothing to make anyone forget the fact that I'm about as likely to clone a fruit fly as I am to use animal-tested hair products.

"Um," I said. "Can't you make it a little more . . . I don't know . . . sexy?"

Grandmère and Sebastiano exchanged looks. "Sexy?" Grandmère echoed, with an evil laugh. "How? By making it lower cut? But you haven't got anything there to show!"

Now, seriously. I would expect to hear this kind of thing from the cheerleaders at school, who have made demeaning other people—especially me—a sort of new Olympic sport. But what kind of person says things like this to her only grandchild? I had meant, of course, a side slit, or maybe some fringe. I wasn't asking for anything Jennifer Lopez-ish.

But trust Grandmère to turn it into something like that. Why do I have to be cursed with a grandmother who shaves off her eyebrows and seems to enjoy making light of my inadequacies? Why can't I have a normal grandmother, who bakes me cookies and can't stop bragging to her friends in her bridge club about how wonderful I am?

It was while Grandmère and Sebastiano were cackling to themselves over this great witticism at my expense that my dad abruptly got up and left the table, saying he had to make a call. I suppose it's every man for himself where Grandmère is concerned, but you would think my own father would stick up for me once in a while.

I don't know, maybe I was feeling odd about the giant hole in my tongue (which doesn't even have a nice hypoallergenic stud in it so I can pretend to have done it on purpose to be controversial). I sat there listening to Grandmère and Sebastiano chatter away about how pathetic it was that I would never be able to wear anything strapless, unless some miracle of nature occurred one night that inflated me from a 32A to a 34C, and I couldn't help thinking that probably, given my luck, it will turn out that Sebastiano isn't in town just to design me a dress for my royal introduction, but to kill me so that he can assume the throne of Genovia himself.

Or, as Sebastiano would say, "ass" the throne.

Seriously. That kind of stuff happens on *Baywatch* all the time. You wouldn't believe the number of royal family members Mitch has had to save from assassination.

Like supposing I put on the dress that Sebastiano

has designed for me to wear when I'm introduced to the people of Genovia, and it ends up squeezing me to death, just like that corset Snow White puts on in the original version of the story by the Brothers Grimm. You know, the part they left out of the Disney movie because it was too gruesome.

Anyway, what if the dress squeezes me to death, and then I'm lying in my coffin, looking all pale and queenly, and Michael comes to my funeral and ends up gazing down at me and doesn't realize until right then that he has always loved me?

Then he'll *have* to break up with Judith Gershner.

Hey. It could happen.

Okay, well, probably not, but thinking about that was better than listening to Grandmère and Sebastiano talk about me as if I weren't even there. Seriously. I was roused from my pleasant little fantasy about Michael pining for me for the rest of his life by Sebastiano saying suddenly, "She has bute bone struck," which, when I realized I was the *she* he was referring to, I took to be a compliment about my bone structure.

Only a second later it wasn't such a compliment when he went, "I put makeup on her that make her look like a mod."

Implying I don't look like a model without makeup (although of course I don't).

Grandmère certainly wasn't about to come to my defense, however. She was feeding bits of her leftover veal marsala to Rommel, who was sitting on her lap, shivering as usual, since all of his fur has fallen out due to canine allergies.

"I wouldn't count on her father letting you," she said to Sebastiano. "Phillipe is hopelessly old-fashioned."

Which is so the pot calling the kettle black! I mean, Grandmère still thinks that cats go around trying to suck the breath out of their owners while they are sleeping. Seriously. She is always trying to convince me to give Fat Louie away.

So while Grandmère was going on about how old-fashioned her son is, I got up and joined him on the balcony.

He was checking his messages on his cell phone. He's supposed to play racquetball tomorrow with the prime minister of France, who is in town for the same summit as the emperor of Japan.

"Mia," he said, when he saw me. "What are you doing out here? It's freezing. Go back inside."

"I will, in a minute," I said. I stood there next to him and looked out over the city. It really is kind of awe-inspiring, the view of Manhattan from the penthouse of the Plaza Hotel. I mean, you look at all those lights in all those windows, and you think, for each light there's probably at least one person, but maybe even more, maybe even like ten people, and that's, well, pretty mind-boggling.

I've lived in Manhattan my whole life. But it still impresses me.

Anyway, while I was standing there looking at all the lights, I suddenly realized that one of them probably belonged to Judith Gershner. Judith was probably sitting in her room right this moment cloning something new. A pigeon, or whatever. I got yet another flashback of her and Michael looking down at me after I'd split open my tongue. Hmmm, let me see: girl who can clone things, or girl who bit her own tongue? I don't know, who would *you* choose?

My dad must have noticed something was wrong, since he went, "Look, I know Sebastiano is a bit much, but just put up with him for the next couple of weeks. For my sake."

"I wasn't thinking about Sebastiano," I said sadly.

My dad made this grunting noise, but he made no move to go back inside, even though it was about forty degrees out there, and my dad, well, he's completely bald. I could see that the tips of his ears were getting red with cold, but still he didn't budge. He didn't even have a coat on, just another one of his charcoal-gray Armani suits.

I figured this was invitation enough to go on. You see, ordinarily my dad is not who I would go to first if I had a problem. Not that we're not close. It's just that, you know, he's a guy.

On the other hand, he's had a lot of experience in

the romance department, so I figured he might just be able to offer some insight into this particular dilemma.

"Dad," I said. "What do you do if you like someone, but they don't, you know, know it?"

My dad went, "If Kenny doesn't know you like him by now, then I'm afraid he's never going to get the message. Haven't you been out with him every weekend since Halloween?"

This is the problem with having a bodyguard who is on your father's payroll: All of your personal business totally gets discussed behind your back.

"I'm not talking about Kenny, Dad," I said. "It's someone else. Only like I said, he doesn't know I like him."

"What's wrong with Kenny?" my dad wanted to know. "I like Kenny."

Of course my dad likes Kenny. Because the chances of me and Kenny ever getting past first base are like, nil. What father doesn't want his teenage daughter to date a guy like that?

But if my dad has any serious hope of keeping the Genovian throne in the hands of the Renaldos, and not allowing it to slip into Sebastiano's control, he had better get over the whole Kenny thing, because I'm pretty sure that Kenny and I will not be doing any procreating. In this lifetime, anyway.

"Dad," I said. "Forget Kenny, okay? Kenny and I

are just friends. I'm talking about someone else."

My dad was looking over the side of the balcony railing like he wanted to spit. Not that he ever would. I don't think. "Do I know him? This someone else, I mean?"

I hesitated. I've never really admitted to anyone out loud that I have a crush on Michael. Really. Not to anybody. I mean, who could I tell? Lilly would just make fun of me, or worse, tell Michael. And Mom, well, she's got her own problems.

"It's Lilly's brother," I said in a rush, to get it over with.

My dad looked alarmed. "Isn't he in college?"

"Not yet," I said. "He's going in the fall." When he still looked alarmed, I said, "Don't worry, Dad. I don't stand a chance. Michael is very smart. He'd never like someone like me."

Then my dad got all offended. It was like he couldn't figure out which to be, worried about my liking a senior, or angry that that senior didn't like me back.

"What do you mean, he'd never like someone like you?" my father demanded. "What's wrong with you?"

"Duh, Dad," I said. "I practically flunked Algebra, remember? Michael is going to an Ivy League school in the fall, for crying out loud. What would he want with a girl like me?"

Now my dad was *really* annoyed: "You may take

after your mother as far as your aptitude with numbers is concerned, but you take after me in every other respect."

This was surprising to hear. I stuck out my chin and tried to believe it. "Yeah," I said.

"And you and I, Mia, are not unintelligent," my dad went on. "If you want this Michael fellow, you must let him know it."

"You think I should just go up to him and be like, 'Hey, I like you'?"

My dad shook his head in disgust. "No, no, no," he said. "Of course you must be more subtle than that. Tell him by *showing* how you feel."

"Oh," I said. I may take after my father in every respect except my math aptitude, but I had no idea what he was talking about.

"We'd better get back in," my father said. "Or your grandmother will suspect us of plotting against her."

So what else is new? Grandmère is always suspecting somebody of plotting something against her. She thinks the launderers at the Plaza are plotting against her. She blames the soap they use on their linens for making all of Rommel's fur fall out.

Reminded of plots, I asked my dad, "Do you think Sebastiano's plotting to kill me so he can ascend the throne himself?"

My dad made a strangled noise, but he managed not to burst out laughing. I guess that wouldn't have seemed very princely.

"No, Mia," he said. "I do not."

But my dad, he really doesn't have much of an imagination. I have decided to stay on alert about Sebastiano, just in case.

My mom just poked her head into my room to say that Kenny is on the phone for me.

I suppose he wants to ask me to the Nondenominational Winter Dance. Really, it is about time.

Sunday, December 7, 11 p.m.

Okay. I am in shock. Kenny so did NOT ask me to the Nondenominational Winter Dance. Instead, this is how our conversation went:

Me: Hello?
Kenny: Hi, Mia. It's Kenny.
Me: Oh, hi, Kenny. What's the matter?

Kenny sounded funny, which is why I asked.

Kenny: Well, I just wanted to see if you were
         okay. I mean, if your tongue was okay.
Me: It's a little better, I guess.
Kenny: Because I was really worried. You know. I
         really, really didn't mean to—
Me: Kenny, I know. It was just an accident.

This is when I started realizing I'd asked my dad the wrong question. I should have asked him what's the best way to break up with somebody, not what's the best way to let someone know you like them.

Anyway, to get back to what Kenny said:

Kenny: Well, I just wanted to call and wish you a
         good night. And say that I hope you feel

better. And also to let you know . . . well,
Mia, that I love you.

Me: . . . .

I didn't say anything right away, because I was completely FREAKED OUT!!!! It wasn't exactly as if it
happened out of the blue, because we are sort of going
out, after all.

But still, what kind of guy calls a girl on the phone
and says I love you??? Except for weird psycho stalkers?
And Kenny's not a weird psycho stalker. He's just Kenny.
So what's he doing calling me on the phone and telling
me he loves me????

And then, brilliant me, here's what I do. Because
he was still on the phone, waiting for an answer, and all.
So I go:

Me: Um, okay.

Um, okay.
A boy says he loves me, and this is how I respond:
"Um, okay." Oh, yeah, good thing my future career
lies in the diplomatic corps.

So then, poor Kenny, he's like waiting for some
response other than "Um, okay," as anybody would.

But I am perfectly incapable of giving him one.
Instead, I just go:

Me: Well, see you tomorrow.

AND I HUNG UP!!!!!
Oh, my God, I am the meanest, most ungrateful girl
in the world. After Sebastiano kills me, I am going to
burn in hell.
Seriously.

TO DO BEFORE LEAVING FOR GENOVIA

1. Detailed list for Mom and Mr. G: How to care
   for Fat Louie while I am away
2. Stock up on cat food, litter
3. Christmas/Hannukah presents! For:
   Mom—electric breast pump? Check on this.
   Mr. G—new drumsticks
   Dad—book on vegetarianism. He should
   eat better if he wants to keep his cancer in
   remission.
   Lilly—what she always wants, blank videotapes
   for her show
   Lars—See if Prada makes a shoulder holster
   that would fit his Glock
   Kenny—gloves? Something NON-romantic
   Fat Louie—catnip ball
   Grandmère—What do you get for the woman
   who has everything, including an eighty-nine-
   carat sapphire pendant given to her by the
   Sultan of Brunei? Soap on a rope?
4. Break up with Kenny. . . . Only how can I? He
   LOVES me.

But not enough to ask me to the Nondenominational Winter Dance, I've noticed.

Monday, December 8, Homeroom

Lilly doesn't believe me about Kenny calling and saying he loves me. I told her in the car on the way to school this morning (thank God Michael had a dentist appointment and wasn't there. I would sooner die than discuss my love life in front of him. It's bad enough having to discuss it in front of my bodyguard. If I had to discuss it in front of this person I've been worshiping for half my life, I think I'd probably go completely borderline personality disorder).

Anyway, so Lilly went, "I categorically refuse to believe Kenny would do something like that."

"Lilly," I said. I had to keep my voice down so the driver wouldn't hear. "I am dead serious. He told me he loves me. *I love you.* That is what he said. It was completely random and weird."

"He probably didn't say that. He probably said something else, and you misunderstood him."

"Oh, what? I *glove* you?"

"Well, of course not," Lilly said. "That doesn't even make any sense."

"Well, then what? What could Kenny have said that sounded like *I love you*, but wasn't *I love you*?"

Lilly got mad then. She went, "You know, you have been acting weird about Kenny for the past month. Since the two of you started going out, practically. I don't know what's wrong with you. All I ever heard before was 'Why don't I have a boyfriend? How come everybody I know has a boyfriend but me? When am I going to get a boyfriend?' And now you've got one and you aren't the least bit appreciative of him."

Even though what she was saying was true, I acted offended, because I have been trying really hard not to let the fact that I am not in love with Kenny show.

"That is so false," I said. "I completely appreciate Kenny."

"Oh, yeah? I think the truth of the matter is, you, Mia, simply aren't ready to have a boyfriend."

Boy did I see red after *that* remark.

"*Me?* Not ready to have a boyfriend? Are you kidding? I've been waiting my whole life to have a boyfriend!"

"Well, if that's true"—Lilly was looking very superior—"why won't you let him kiss you on the lips?"

"Where did you hear *that?*" I demanded.

"Kenny told Boris, of course, who told me."

"Oh, great," I said, trying to remain calm. "So now our boyfriends are talking about us behind our backs. And you're condoning this?"

"Of course not," Lilly said. "But I do find it intriguing, from a psychological point of view."

This is the problem with being best friends with someone whose parents are psychiatrists. Everything you do is interesting to them from a psychological point of view.

"Where I let anybody kiss me," I exploded, "is *my* business! Not yours, and not Boris's, either."

"Well," Lilly said. "I'm just saying, if Kenny did say what you say he said—you know, the L word—then maybe he said it because he can't express the depth of his feelings any other way. You know. Other than *verbally*. Since you won't *let* him, physically."

So I suppose that technically I should be thankful that Kenny chose merely to *say* the words I love you, rather than enacting them physically, which, God knows, might have actually involved his tongue.

Oh, God, I don't even want to think about it anymore.

Monday, December 8, Homeroom

They just passed out the final exam schedules. Here is mine:

FINAL EXAM SCHEDULE

December 15
Reading Day

December 16
Periods One and Two

For me, that means the Algebra and English finals will be on the same day. But that's okay. I'm doing pretty good in English. Well, except for that sentence diagramming thing. As if I'll ever need to do *that* in my future role as princess of the smallest nation in Europe.

Unfortunately, Algebra, I am told, I will probably need to know. DAMN!

December 17
Periods Three and Four

World Civ: Easy. I mean, Grandmère has told me enough stories about post–World War II Europe for me to pass any test. I probably know more about it than the teacher. And PE? How can you give a final in PE?

We already had the Presidential Fitness Test (I did okay on everything but the V-sit reach).

December 18
Periods Five, Six, and Seven

Gifted and Talented? No exam there. They don't give finals in classes that are basically study hall. That will be a snap. I have French sixth period. I do okay in oral, not so great in written. Fortunately Tina's in the same class. Maybe we can study together.

But I have Bio seventh period. That won't be so easy. The only reason I'm not flunking Bio is because of Kenny. He slips me most of the answers.

And if I break up with him, that will be the end of that.

December 19
Nondenominational Winter Carnival and Dance

The Winter Carnival should be fun. All the different school clubs and groups are going to have booths, with traditional winter fare, like hot cider. This will be followed in the evening by the dance I am supposed to go to with Kenny. If he ever asks me to it, I mean.

Unless, of course, I do the right thing and break up with him.

In which case, I won't be able to go at all, because you can't go without a date.

I wish Sebastiano would just hurry up and off me already.

WHY???? WHY can't I ever remember my Algebra notebook?????

FIRST—Evaluate exponents

SECOND—Multiply and divide in order, left to right

THIRD—Perform addition and subtraction in order, left to right

EXAMPLE: $2 \times 3 - 15 \div 5 = 6 - 3 = 3$

Oh, God. Lana Weinberger just tossed me a note.

What now? This can't be good. Lana's had it out for me forever. Don't ask me why. I mean, I could kind of understand her resenting me for when Josh Richter asked me to the Cultural Diversity Dance instead of her. But he only asked me because of the princess thing—and they got back together right after. Besides, Lana hated me long before that.

So I open the note. Here's what it says:

I heard what happened to you at the skating rink this weekend. Guess the BF is going to have to wait a little longer if he wants to see any tongue action, huh?

Oh, my God. Does *everyone* in the entire school know that Kenny and I have not yet French kissed?

It is all Kenny's fault, of course.

What next? The cover of the *Post*?

I'm telling you, if our parents knew what actually goes on every day in the typical American high school, they would totally opt for homeschooling.

It's clear what I have to do.

I've always known it, of course, and if it hadn't been for, you know, the dance, I would have done it long before now.

But it is clear now that I cannot afford to wait until after the dance. I should have done it last night when he called, but you can't really do something like that over the phone. Well, I mean, a girl like Lana Weinberger probably could, but not me.

No, I don't think I can put it off another day: I have got to break up with Kenny. I simply cannot continue living this lie.

Fortunately, I do have the support of at least one person in this plan: Tina Hakim Baba.

I didn't want to tell her. I didn't plan on telling anybody. But it all sort of slipped out today in the girls' room between second and third periods while Tina was putting on her eye makeup. Her dad won't let her wear makeup, you see, so Tina has to wait until she gets to school to put it on. She has a deal with her bodyguard, Wahim. Tina won't tell her parents how much Wahim flirts with Mademoiselle Klein, our French teacher, if Wahim doesn't tell Mr. and Mrs. Hakim Baba about Tina's Maybelline addiction.

Anyway, all of a sudden I just couldn't take it anymore, and I ended up telling Tina what Kenny said last night on the phone—

And a lot more than that actually.

But first the part about Kenny's phone call:

Unlike Lilly, *Tina* believed me.

But Tina also had the totally wrong reaction. She thought it was great.

"Oh, my God, Mia, you are so lucky," she kept saying. "I wish Dave would tell me he loves me! I mean, I know he is fully committed to our relationship, but his idea of romance is paying to have my fries super-sized at Mickey D's."

This was so not the kind of support I was looking for.

"But, Tina," I said. I felt Tina, with her extensive reading of romances, would understand. "The thing is, I don't love him."

Tina widened her mascaraed eyes at me. "You don't?"

"No," I said, miserably. "I mean, I really like him, as a friend. But I'm not in love, or anything. Not with him."

"Oh, God," Tina said, reaching out and grabbing my wrist. "There's someone else, isn't there?"

We only had a few minutes before the bell rang. We both had to get to class.

And yet, for some reason, I chose this moment to make my big confession. I don't know why. Maybe since I'd already spilled it to my dad, it didn't seem too hard to tell someone else, especially Tina. Also, I can't stop thinking about what my dad said. You know, about showing the guy I like how I feel. Tina, I felt, was the only person I knew who would know how to help me do that.

So I went, "Yes."

Tina nearly spilled her cosmetics bag, she was so excited.

"I knew it!" she yelled. "I knew there was a reason you wouldn't let him kiss you!"

My jaw dropped. "*You* know about that, too?"

"Well." Tina shrugged. "Kenny told Dave, who told me."

Jeez! What's that Oprah always complaining about, about how men aren't in touch with their emotions, and don't share enough? It sounds to me like Kenny's been doing enough sharing recently to make up for several centuries' worth of masculine reticence.

"So who is he?" Tina asked, all eager as she packed up her eyelash curler and lipliner. "The guy you like?"

I went, "It doesn't matter. Besides, the whole thing is completely futile. He sort of has a girlfriend. I think."

Tina whipped her head around to look at me, making her thick, black braid smack her in her own face, which is chubby, but in a good way.

"It's Michael, isn't it?" she demanded, grabbing my arm again. She was holding on so tight it hurt.

My instinct, of course, was to deny it. In fact, I

even opened my mouth, all set to have the word *No* come out of it.

But then I was like, Why? Why should I deny it to Tina? Tina wouldn't tell anyone. And Tina might be able to help me.

So instead of saying No, I took a deep breath, and said, "If you tell anyone, I'll kill you, understand? KILL YOU."

Tina did a strange thing then. She let go of my arm and started jumping up and down in a circle.

"I knew it, I knew it, I knew it," she said, as she jumped. Then she stopped jumping and grabbed my arm again. "Oh, Mia, I always thought you two would make the cutest couple. I mean, I like Kenny and all, but he's, you know." She wrinkled up her nose. "Not Michael."

If I had thought it felt strange last night telling my dad the truth about my feelings for Michael, that was nothing—NOTHING—compared to how it felt to be telling someone my own age. The fact that Tina hadn't burst out laughing or gone, "Yeah, right," in a sarcastic way meant more to me than I ever would have expected.

And the fact that she seemed to understand—even applaud—my feelings for Michael made me want to fling my arms around her and give her a great big hug.

Only there was no time for that, since the bell was about to ring.

Instead, I gushed, "Really? You really don't think it's stupid?"

"Duh," Tina said. "Michael is *hot*. *And* he's a senior." Then she looked troubled. "But what about Kenny? And Judith?"

"I know," I said, my shoulders slumping in a manner that would have caused Grandmère to rap me on the back of the head, if she'd seen them. "Tina, I don't know what to do."

Tina's dark eyebrows furrowed with concentration. "I think I read a book where this happened once," she said. "*Listen to My Heart*, it was called, I think. If I could just remember how they resolved everything—"

But before she could remember, the bell rang. We were both totally late to class.

But if you ask me, it was worth it. Because now, at least, I don't have to worry alone. I have somebody else worrying with me.

Lunch was a disaster.

Considering that everybody in the entire school seems to know, in the minutest detail, exactly what I've been doing—or not doing—with my tongue lately, I guess I shouldn't have been surprised. But it was even worse than I could have imagined.

That's because I ran into Michael at the salad bar. I was creating my usual chickpea-and-pinto-bean pyramid when I saw him headed for the burger grill (despite my best efforts, both Moscovitzes remain stubbornly carnivorous).

Seriously, all I did was say "Fine" when he asked how I was doing. You know, on account of how last time he saw me, I was bleeding out of the mouth (what a nice picture that must have been. I am so glad that I have been able to maintain an appearance of dignity and beauty at all times in front of the man I love).

Anyway, then I asked him, just to be polite, you know, how his dentist appointment went. What happened next was not my fault.

Which was that Michael started telling me about how he'd had to have this cavity filled, and that his lips were still numb from the novocaine. Seeing as how I have experienced a certain amount of sensation-deadening, what with my gouged tongue, I could relate to this, so I just sort of, you know, *looked* at Michael's lips while he was talking, which I have never really done before. I mean, I have looked at other parts of Michael's body (particularly when he comes into the kitchen in the morning with no shirt on, like he does every time I have a sleepover at Lilly's). But I've never really looked at his lips. You know. Up close.

Michael actually has very nice lips. Not thin lips, like mine. I don't know if you should say this about a boy's lips, but Michael's lips look like if you kissed them, they'd be very soft.

It was while I was noticing this about Michael's lips that the very bad thing happened: I was looking at them, you know, and wondering if they'd be soft to kiss, and as I looked, I sort of actually pictured us kissing, you know, in my head. And right then I got this very warm feeling—the one they talk about in all of Tina's romance novels—and RIGHT THEN was when Kenny went by on his way to get his usual lunch: Coke and an ice-cream sandwich.

I know Kenny can't read my mind—if he could, he totally would have broken up with me by now—but maybe he caught some hint as to what I was thinking, and that's why he didn't say *Hi* back, when Michael and I said "Hi" to him.

Well, that and the whole part where I said, "Um, okay," after he said he loved me.

Kenny must have known something was up, if my face was anywhere near as red-hot as it felt. Maybe *that*'s why he didn't say *Hi* back. Because I was looking so guilty. I'd certainly *felt* guilty. I mean, there I was, looking at another guy's lips and wondering what it would be like to kiss them, and my boyfriend goes walking by.

I am so going to bad-girl hell when I die.

You know what I wish? I wish everyone *could* read my mind. Because then Kenny would never have asked me out. He'd have known I don't think of him that way. And Lilly wouldn't make fun of me for not letting Kenny kiss me. She would know the reason I don't is that I'm in love with someone else.

The bad part is, she'd know who that someone else is.

And that someone probably won't even speak to me again, because it's totally uncool for a senior to go out with a freshman. Especially one who can't go anywhere without a bodyguard.

Besides, I'm almost positive he's going out with Judith Gershner, because after he came back from the grill, he went and sat down next to her.

So that settles that.

I wish I were leaving for Genovia tomorrow instead of in two weeks.

In spite of that disastrous incident at lunch, I had a pretty good time in Gifted and Talented. In fact, it was almost like old times again. I mean, before we all started going out with each other and everyone became so obsessed with the inner workings of my mouth, and all that.

Mrs. Hill spent the whole class period in the teachers' lounge across the hall, yelling at American Express on the phone, leaving us free to do what we usually do during her class . . . whatever we wanted. For instance, those of us who, like Lilly's boyfriend Boris, wanted to work on our individual projects (Boris's is learning to play some new sonata on his violin), which is what Gifted and Talented class is supposedly for, did so.

Those of us, however, like Lilly and me, who did not want to work on our individual projects (mine is studying for Algebra; Lilly's is working on her cable access TV show) did not.

This was especially satisfying, because Lilly had completely forgotten about the whole kissing thing between Kenny and me. The reason for this is that now she's mad at Mrs. Spears, her honors English teacher, who shot down her term paper proposal.

It really was unfair of Mrs. Spears to turn it down, because it was actually very well thought out, and quite creative. I made a copy of it:

HOW TO SURVIVE HIGH SCHOOL
by Lilly Moscovitz

Having spent the past two months locked in that institution of secondary education commonly referred to as high school, I feel that I am a qualified authority on the subject. From pep rallies to morning announcements, I have observed high-school life and all of its complexities. Sometime in the next four years, I will be granted my freedom from this festering hellhole, and then I will publish my carefully compiled *High School Survival Guide*.

Little did my peers and teachers know that as they went about their daily routines, I was recording their activities for study by future generations. With my handy guide, every ninth grader's sojourn in high school can be a little more fruitful. Students of the future will learn that the way to settle their differences with their peers is not through violence, but through the sale of a really scathing screenplay—featuring characters based on those very individuals who tormented them all those years—to a major Hollywood movie studio. That, not a Molotov cocktail, is the path to true glory.

Here, for your reading pleasure, are a few examples of the topics I will explore in *How to Survive High School*, by Lilly Moscovitz:

1. High-School Romance, or How I Cannot Open My Locker Because Two Oversexed Adolescents are

Leaning Up Against It, Making Out
2. Cafeteria Food: Can Corndogs Legally Be Listed as a Meat Product?
3. How to Communicate with the Subhumans Who Populate the Hallways
4. Guidance Counselors: Who Do They Think They're Kidding?
5. Get Ahead by Forging: The Art of the Hall Pass

Does that sound good, or what? Now look what Mrs. Spears had to say about it:

Lilly—Sorry as I am to hear that your experience thus far at AEHS has not been a positive one, I am afraid I am going to have to make it worse by asking you to find another topic for your term paper. A for creativity, as usual, however.

—Mrs. Spears

Can you believe that? Talk about unfair! Lilly's been censored! By rights, her proposal ought to have brought the school's administration to its knees. Lilly says she is appalled by the fact that, considering how much our tuition costs, this is the kind of support we can expect from our teachers. Then I reminded her that that isn't true of Mr. Gianini, who really goes beyond the call of duty by staying after school every day to conduct help sessions for people like me, who aren't doing so well in Algebra.

Lilly says Mr. Gianini probably only started pulling that staying-after-school thing so that he could ingratiate himself to my mother, and now he can't stop, because then she'll realize it was all just a setup and divorce him.

I don't believe that, however. I think Mr. G would have stayed after school to help me whether he was dating my mom or not. He's that kind of guy.

Anyway, the upshot of it all is that now Lilly has launched another one of her famous campaigns. This is actually a good thing, as it will keep her mind off me and where I am putting (or not putting) my lips. Here's how it started:

Lilly:	The real problem with this school isn't the teachers. It's the apathy of the student body. For instance, let's say we wanted to stage a walkout.
Me:	A walkout?
Lilly:	You know. We all get up and walk out of the school at the same time.
Me:	Just because Mrs. Spears turned down your term paper proposal?
Lilly:	No, Mia. Because she's trying to usurp our individuality by forcing us to bend to corporate feudalism. Again.
Me:	Oh. And how is she doing that?

Lilly:	By censoring us when we are at our most fertile, creatively speaking.
Boris:	(leaning out of the supply closet, where Lilly made him go when he started practicing his latest sonata) Fertile? Did someone say *fertile*?
Lilly:	Get back in the closet, Boris. Michael, can you send a mass e-mail tonight to the entire student body, declaring a walkout tomorrow at eleven?
Michael:	(working on the booth he and Judith Gershner and the rest of the Computer Club are going to have up at the Winter Carnival) I can, but I won't.
Lilly:	WHY NOT?
Michael:	Because it was your turn to empty the dishwasher last night, but you weren't home, so I had to do it.
Lilly:	But I TOLD Mom I had to go down to the studio to edit the last few finishing touches on this week's show!

Lilly's TV program, *Lilly Tells It Like It Is*, is now one of the highest-ranked shows on Manhattan cable. Of course, it's public access, so it's not like she's making any money off it, but a bunch of the major networks picked up this interview she did of me one night when I was half asleep and played it. I thought it was stupid, but I guess a lot of other people thought it was good, because now Lilly gets tons of viewer mail, whereas before the only mail she got was from her stalker, Norman.

Michael: Look, if you're having time-management issues, don't take it out on me. Just don't expect me to meekly do your bidding, especially when you already owe me one.

Me: Lilly, no offense, but I don't think this week's a good time for a walkout, anyway. I mean, after all, it's almost finals.

Lilly: SO???

Me: So some of us really need to stay in class. I can't afford to miss any review sessions. My grades are bad enough as it is.

Michael: Really? I thought you were doing better in Algebra.

Me: If you call a D plus better.

Michael: Aw, come on. You have to be making better than a D plus. Your mom is married to your Algebra teacher!

Me: So? That doesn't mean anything. You know Mr. G doesn't play favorites.

Michael: I would think he'd cut his own stepdaughter a little slack, is all.

Lilly: WOULD YOU TWO PLEASE PAY ATTENTION TO THE SITUATION

AT HAND, WHICH IS THE FACT THAT THIS SCHOOL IS IN VITAL NEED OF SERIOUS REFORM?

Fortunately at that moment the bell rang, so no walkout tomorrow as far as I know. Which is a good thing, because I really need the extra study time.

You know, it's funny about Mrs. Spears not liking Lilly's term paper proposal, because she was very enthusiastic about my proposal, *A Case Against Christmas Trees: Why We Must Curtail the Pagan Ritual of Chopping Down Pine Trees Every December if We Are Going to Repair the Ozone Layer.*

And my IQ isn't anywhere near as high as Lilly's.

Monday, December 8, Bio

Kenny just passed me the following note:

> *Mia—I hope what I said to you last night didn't make you feel uncomfortable. I just wanted you to know how I feel.*
>
> > Sincerely,
> > Kenny

Oh, God. *Now* what am I supposed to do? He's sitting here next to me, waiting for an answer. In fact, that's what he thinks I'm writing right now. An answer.

What do I say?

Maybe this is my perfect opportunity to break up with him. *I'm sorry, Kenny, but I don't feel the same way—let's just be friends.* Is that what I should say?

It's just that I don't want to hurt his feelings, you know? And he is my Bio partner. I mean, whatever happens, I am going to have to sit next to him for the next two weeks. And I would much rather have a Bio partner who likes me than one who hates me.

And what about the dance? I mean, if I break up with him, who am I going to go to the Nondenominational Winter Dance with? I know it is horrible to think things like this, but this is the first dance in the history of my life to which I already have a date.

Well, I mean, if he'd ever get around to asking me.

And how about that final, huh? Our Bio final, I mean. No way am I going to be able to pass without Kenny's notes. NO WAY.

But what else can I do? I mean, considering what happened today at the salad bar.

This is it. Good-bye, date for the Nondenominational Winter Dance. Hello, Friday-night television.

Dear Kenny,
    It isn't that I don't think of you as a very dear friend. It's just that—

Monday, December 8, 3 p.m., Mr. Gianini's Algebra review

Okay, so the bell rang before I had time to finish my note.

That doesn't mean I'm not going to tell Kenny exactly how I feel. I totally am. Tonight, as a matter of fact. I don't care if it's cruel to do something like that over the phone. I just can't take it anymore.

HOMEWORK

Algebra: review questions at the end of Chapters 1–3
English: term paper
World Civ: review questions at the end of Chapters 1–4
G & T: none
French: review questions at the end of Chapters 1–3
Biology: review questions at the end of Chapters 1–5

All right. So I didn't break up with him.

I totally meant to.

And it wasn't even because I didn't have the heart to do it over the phone, either.

It was something *Grandmère*, of all people, said.

Not that I feel right about it. Not breaking up with him, I mean. It's just that after Algebra review, I had to go to the showroom where Sebastiano is flogging his latest creations, so that he could have his flunkies take my measurements for my dress. Grandmère was going on about how from now on, I should really only wear clothes by Genovian designers, to show my patriotism, or whatever. Which is going to be hard, because, uh, there's only one Genovian clothing designer that I know of, and that's Sebastiano. And let's just say he doesn't make very much out of denim.

But whatever. I so had more important things to worry about than my spring wardrobe.

Which I guess Grandmère must have caught on to, because midway through Sebastiano's description of the beading he was going to have sewn onto my gown's bodice, Grandmère shouted, "Amelia, what is the matter with you?"

I must have jumped about a foot in the air. "What?"

"Sebastiano asked if you prefer a sweetheart or square-cut neckline."

I stared at her blankly. "Neckline for what?"

Grandmère gave me the evil eye. She does this quite frequently. That's why my father, even though he has the neighboring hotel suite, never stops by during my princess lessons.

"Sebastiano," my grandmother said. "You will please leave the princess and me for a moment."

And Sebastiano—who was wearing a new pair of leather pants, these in a tangerine color (the new gray, he told me; and white, you might be surprised to know, is the new black)—bowed and left the room, followed by the slinky ladies who'd been taking my measurements.

"Now," Grandmère said imperiously. "Something is clearly troubling you, Amelia. What is it?"

"It's nothing," I said, turning all red. I knew I was turning all red because: a) I could feel it, and b) I could see my reflection in the three full-length mirrors in front of me.

"It is not nothing." Grandmère took in a healthy drag from her Gitanes, even though I have asked her repeatedly not to smoke in my presence, as breathing secondhand smoke can cause just as much lung damage as actually smoking. "What is it? Trouble at home? Your mother and the math teacher fighting already, I suppose. Well, I never expected *that* marriage to last. Your mother is much too flighty."

I have to admit, I kind of snapped when she said that. Grandmère is always putting my mother down, even though Mom has raised me pretty much single-handedly and I certainly haven't gotten pregnant or shot anyone yet.

"For your information," I said, "my mom and Mr. Gianini are blissfully happy together. I wasn't thinking about them at all."

"What is it, then?" Grandmère asked in a bored voice.

"Nothing," I practically yelled. "I just—well, I was thinking about the fact that I have to break up with my boyfriend tonight, that's all. Not that it's any of your business."

Instead of taking offense at my tone, which any self-respecting grandparent would have found insolent, Grandmère only took a sip of her drink and suddenly looked way interested.

"Oh?" she said, in a totally different tone of voice—the same tone of voice she uses when someone mentions a stock tip she thinks might be useful for her portfolio. "What boyfriend is this?"

God, what did I ever do to be cursed with such a grandmother? Seriously. Lilly and Michael's grandma remembers the names of all their friends, makes them rugelach all the time, and always worries that they're not getting enough to eat, even though their parents, the Drs. Moscovitz, are wholly reliable at bringing home groceries, or at least ordering out.

Me? I get the grandma with the hairless poodle and

the nine-carat diamond rings whose greatest joy in life is to torture me.

And why is that, anyway? I mean, why does Grandmère love to torture me so much? I've never done anything to her. Nothing except be her only grandchild, anyway. And it isn't exactly like I go around advertising how I feel about her. You know, I've never actually *told* her I think she's a mean old lady who contributes to the destruction of the environment by wearing fur coats and smoking filterless French cigarettes.

"Grandmère," I said, trying to remain calm. "I have only one boyfriend. His name is Kenny." I've only told you about fifty thousand times, I added, in my head.

"I thought this Kenny person was your Biology partner," Grandmère said, after taking a sip of her sidecar, her favorite drink.

"He is," I said, a little surprised that she'd managed to remember something like that. "He's also my boyfriend. Only last night he went completely schizo on me, and told me he loves me."

Grandmère patted Rommel, who was sitting in her lap looking miserable (his habitual expression), on the head.

"And what is so wrong," Grandmère wanted to know, "about a boy who says he loves you?"

"Nothing," I said. "Only I'm not in love with him, see? So it wouldn't be fair of me to, you know, lead him on."

Grandmère raised her painted-on eyebrows. "I don't see why not."

How had I ever gotten into this conversation? "Because, Grandmère. People just don't go around *doing* things like that. Not nowadays."

"Is that so? Well, my observations of people are to the contrary. Except, of course, if one happens to be in love with someone else. Then shedding an unwanted suitor might be considered wise, so that one can make oneself available to the man one truly desires." She eyed me. "Is there someone like that in your life, Amelia? Someone—ahem—special?"

"No." I lied, automatically.

Grandmère snorted. "You're lying."

"No, I'm not." I lied again.

"Indeed you are. I oughtn't tell you this, but I suppose as it is a bad habit for a future monarch, you ought to be made aware of it, so that in the future, you can try to prevent it: When you lie, Amelia, your nostrils flare."

I threw my hands up to my nose. "They do not!"

"Indeed," Grandmère said, clearly enjoying herself immensely. "If you do not believe me, look in the mirror."

I turned around to face the nearby full-length mirrors. Taking my hands from my face, I examined my nose. My nostrils weren't flaring. She was crazy.

"I'll ask you again, Amelia," Grandmère said, in a

lazy voice, from her chair. "Are you in love with anyone right now?"

"No." I lied, automatically. . . .

And my nostrils flared right out!

Oh, my God! All these years I've been lying, and it turns out whenever I do, my nostrils totally give me away! All anyone has to do is look at my nose when I talk, and they'll know for sure whether or not I'm telling the truth.

How could no one have pointed this out to me before? And Grandmère—Grandmère, of all people—was the one who figured it out! Not my mother, with whom I've lived for fourteen years. Not my best friend, whose IQ is higher than Einstein's.

No. Grandmère.

If this got out, my life was over.

"Fine," I cried dramatically, spinning away from the mirror to face her. "All right, yes. Yes, I am in love with somebody else. Are you happy now?"

Grandmère raised her painted-on eyebrows.

"No need to shout, Amelia," she said, with what I might have taken for amusement in anyone other than her. "Who might this special someone be?"

"Oh, no," I said, holding out both my hands. If it wouldn't have been totally rude, I'd have made a little cross out of my index fingers and held it up toward her—that's how much she scares me. And if you think about it, with her tattooed eyeliner, she does look a little like Nosferatu. "You are not getting that information out of me."

Grandmère stamped out her cigarette in the crystal ashtray Sebastiano had provided, and went, "Very well. I take it, then, that the gentleman in question does not return your ardor?"

There was no point in lying to her. Not now. Not with my nostrils.

My shoulders sagged. "No. He likes this other girl. This really smart girl who knows how to clone fruit flies."

Grandmère snorted. "A useful talent. Well, never mind that now. I don't suppose, Amelia, that you are acquainted with the expression dirty dishwater is better than none?"

I guess she must have been able to tell from my perplexed expression that this was one I hadn't heard before, since she went on, "Do not throw away this Kenny until you have managed to secure someone better."

I stared at her, horrified. Really, my grandmother has said—and done—some pretty cold things in her time, but this one took the cake.

"Secure someone better?" I couldn't believe she actually meant what I thought she meant. "You mean I shouldn't break up with Kenny until I've got someone else?"

Grandmère lit another cigarette. "But of course."

"But Grandmère." I swear to God, sometimes I can't figure out if she's human or some kind of alien life force sent down from some other planet to spy on us. "You can't do that. You can't just string a guy along like that, knowing that you don't feel the same way about him that he feels about you."

Grandmère exhaled a long plume of blue smoke. "Why not?"

"Because it's completely unethical!" I shook my head. "No. I'm breaking up with Kenny. Right away. Tonight, as a matter of fact."

Grandmère stroked Rommel under the chin. He looked more miserable than ever, as if instead of stroking him, she was peeling the skin away from his body. He really is the most heinous excuse for a dog I have ever seen.

"That," Grandmère said, "is your prerogative, of course. But allow me to point out to you that if you break off your relationship with this young man, your Biology grade will suffer."

I was shocked. But mostly because this was something I had already thought of myself. I was amazed Grandmère and I had actually shared something.

Which was really the only reason I exclaimed, "Grandmère!"

"Well," Grandmère said, flicking ash from her cigarette into the ashtray. "Isn't it true? You are only making what, a C, in this class? And that is only because that young man allows you to copy his answers to the homework."

"Grandmère!" I squealed again. Because, of course, she was right.

She looked at the ceiling. "Let me see," she said. "With your D in Algebra, if you get anything less than a C in Biology, your grade-point average will take quite a little dip this semester."

"Grandmère." I couldn't believe this. She knew all about my grades! And she was right. She was so right. But still. "I am not going to postpone breaking up with Kenny until after the final. That would be just plain wrong."

"Suit yourself," Grandmère said with a sigh. "But it certainly will be awkward having to sit beside him for the next—how long is it until the end of the semester?— Oh, yes, two weeks. Especially considering the fact that after you break things off with him, he probably won't even speak to you anymore."

God, so true. And not something I hadn't thought of myself. If Kenny got mad enough over me breaking up with him to not want to speak to me anymore, seventh period was going to be plenty unpleasant.

"And what about this dance?" Grandmère rattled the ice in her sidecar. "This Christmas dance?"

"It's not a Christmas dance," I said. "It's a nondenominational—"

Grandmère waved a hand. This spiky charm

bracelet she was wearing tinkled.

"Whatever," she said. "If you stop seeing this young man, who will you go to the dance with?"

"I won't go with anybody," I said, firmly, even though, of course, my heart was breaking at the thought. "I'll just stay home."

"While everyone else has a good time? Really, Amelia, you aren't being at all sensible. What about this other young man?"

"What other young man?"

"The one you claim to be so in love with. Won't he be at this dance with the housefly girl?"

"Fruit fly," I corrected her. "And I don't know. Maybe."

The thought that Michael might ask Judith Gershner to the Nondenominational Winter Dance had never occurred to me. But as soon as Grandmère mentioned it, I felt that same sickening sensation I'd felt at the ice-skating rink when I'd first seen them together: kind of like the time when Lilly and I were crossing Bleecker Street and this Chinese food delivery man crashed into us on his bicycle, and I had the wind completely knocked out of me.

Only this time, it wasn't just my chest that hurt, but my tongue. It had been feeling a lot better, but now it started to throb again.

"It seems to me," Grandmère said, "that one way to get this young man's attention might be to show up at this dance on the arm of this other young man, looking perfectly divine in an original creation by Genovian fashion designer Sebastiano Grimaldi."

I just stared at her. Because she was right. She was so right. Except . . .

"Grandmère," I said. "The guy I like? Yeah, he likes girls who can clone *insects*. Okay? I highly doubt he is going to be impressed by a *dress*."

I didn't mention that I had, of course, just the night before, been hoping that very thing. But almost as if she could read my mind, Grandmère just went, "Hmmm," in this knowing way.

"Suit yourself," she continued. "Still, it seems a bit cruel to me, your breaking things off with this young man at this time of year."

"Why?" I asked, confused. Had Grandmère inadvertently stumbled across some TV channel playing *It's a Wonderful Life*, or something? She had never shown one speck of holiday spirit before now. "Because it's *Christmas*?"

"No," Grandmère said, looking very disgusted with me, I guess over the suggestion that she might ever be moved by the anniversary of the birth of anyone's savior. "Because of your exams. If you truly wish to be kind, I think you might at least wait until after the final exams are over before breaking the poor little fellow's heart."

I had been all ready to argue with whatever excuse

for me not breaking up with Kenny Grandmère came up with next—but this one, I had not expected. I stood there with my mouth hanging open. I know it was hanging open, because I could see it reflected in the three full-length mirrors.

"I cannot imagine," Grandmère went on, "why you do not simply allow him to believe that you return his ardor until your exams are over. Why compound the poor boy's stress? But you must, of course, do what you think is best. I suppose this—er—Kenny is the sort of boy who bounces back easily from rejection. He'll probably do quite well on his exams, in spite of his broken heart."

Oh, God! If she had stabbed a fork in my stomach and twisted my intestines around the tines like spaghetti, she couldn't have made me feel worse. . . .

And, I have to admit, a little relieved. Because of course I can't break up with Kenny now. Never mind my Bio grade and the dance: You can't break up with someone right before finals. It's, like, the meanest thing you can do.

Well, aside from the kind of stuff Lana and her friends pull. You know, girls' locker-room stuff, like going up to someone who is changing and asking her why she wears a bra when she obviously doesn't need one, or making fun of her just because she doesn't happen to like being kissed by her boyfriend. That kind of thing.

So here I am. I *want* to break up with Kenny, but I can't.

I *want* to tell Michael how I feel about him, but I can't do that either.

I can't even quit biting my fingernails. I am going to gross out an entire European nation with my bloody cuticles.

I am a pathetic mess. No wonder in the car this morning—after I accidentally closed the door on Lars's foot—Lilly said that I should really look into getting some therapy, because if there's anybody who needs to find inner harmony between her conscious and her subconscious, it's me.

TO DO BEFORE LEAVING FOR GENOVIA

1. Get cat food, litter for Fat Louie
2. Stop biting fingernails
3. Achieve self-actualization
4. Find inner harmony between conscious and subconscious
5. Break up with Kenny—but not until after finals/Nondenominational Winter Dance

Tuesday, December 9, English

*What was THAT just now in the hallway? Did Kenny
Showalter just say what I think he said to you?*

> Yes. Oh, my God, Shameeka, what am I going to
> do? I'm shaking so hard I can barely write.

*What do you mean, what are you going to do? The boy is
warm for your form, Mia. Go for it.*

> People can't just be allowed to go around saying
> things like that. Especially so loud. Everyone must
> have heard him. Do you think everyone heard him?

*Everybody heard him, all right. You should have seen
Lilly's face. I thought she was going to suffer one of those
synaptic breakdowns she's always talking about.*

> You think EVERYBODY heard him? I mean, like
> the people coming out of the Chemistry lab? Do
> you think they heard?

How could they not? He yelled it pretty loud.

> Were they laughing? The people coming out of
> Chemistry? They weren't laughing, were they?

Most of them were laughing.

> Oh, God! Why was I ever born????

Except Michael. He wasn't laughing.

> He WASN'T? REALLY? Are you pulling my leg?

*No. Why would I do that? And what do you care what
Michael Moscovitz thinks, anyway?*

> I don't. I don't care. What makes you think I
> care?

Um, for one thing because you won't shut up about it.
People shouldn't go around laughing at other
people's misfortunes. That's all.
*I don't see what the big misfortune is. So the guy loves
you? A lot of girls would really like it if their boyfriend
yelled that at them between first and second period.*
Yeah, well, NOT ME!!!!

Use <u>transitive verbs</u> to create brief, vigorous
sentences.

<u>Transitive</u>: He soon regretted his words.
<u>Intransitive</u>: It was not long before he was very
sorry that he had said what he said.

Tuesday, December 9, Bio

Gifted and Talented was so not fun today. Not that Bio is any better, on account of the fact that I am stuck here next to Kenny, who seems to have calmed down a little since this morning.

Still, I really think that people who are not actually enrolled in certain classes have no business showing up in them.

For instance, just because Judith Gershner has study hall for fifth period is no reason that she should be allowed to hang around the Gifted and Talented classroom for fifty minutes during that period. She should never have been let out of study hall in the first place. I don't think she even had a pass.

Not that I would turn her in, or anything. But this kind of flagrant rule-breaking really shouldn't be encouraged. If Lilly is going to go through with this walkout thing, which she is still trying to garner support for, she should really add to her list of complaints the fact that the teachers in this school play favorites. I mean, just because a girl knows how to clone things doesn't mean she should be allowed to roam the school freely any time she wants.

But there she was when I walked in, and there's no doubt about it: Judith Gershner has a total crush on Michael. I don't really know how he feels about her, but she was wearing tan-colored panty hose instead of the black cotton tights she normally wears, so you *know* something is up. No girl wears tan panty hose without a good reason.

And okay, so maybe they are working on their booth for the Winter Carnival, but that is no reason for Judith to drape her arm across the back of Michael's chair like that. Plus he used to help me with my Algebra homework during G and T, but now he can't, because Judith is monopolizing all his time. I would think he might resent the intrusion.

Plus Judith really has no business butting into my private conversations. She hardly even knows me.

But did that stop her from letting me know, when she overheard Lilly's formal apology for not having believed me about Kenny's weird phone call—any doubts about the veracity of which he managed to scatter today with his display of unbridled passion in the third floor hallway—that she feels sorry for him? Oh, no.

"Poor kid," Judith said. "I heard what he said to you in the hallway. I was in the chem lab. What was it again? 'I don't care if you don't feel the same way, Mia, I will always love you,' or something like that?"

I didn't say anything. That's because I was busy picturing how Judith would look with a pencil sticking out of the middle of her forehead.

"It's really sweet," Judith said. "If you think about it. I mean, the guy's clearly got it bad for you."

This is the problem, see. Everyone thinks what Kenny did was so cute and everything. Nobody seems to understand that it wasn't cute. It wasn't cute at all. It was completely humiliating. I don't think I've ever been so embarrassed in my whole life.

And believe me, I've lived through more than my fair share of embarrassing incidents, especially since this whole princess thing started.

But I'm apparently the only person in this entire school who thinks what Kenny did was the least bit wrong.

"He's obviously very in touch with his emotions." Even Lilly was taking Kenny's side in the whole thing. "Unlike *some* people."

I have to say, this makes me so mad when I think about it, because the truth is, ever since I started writing things down in journals, I have gotten very in touch with my emotions. I usually know almost exactly how I feel.

The problem is, I just can't tell anyone.

I don't know who was the most surprised when Michael suddenly came to my defense against his sister—Lilly, Judith Gershner, or me.

"Just because Mia doesn't go around shouting about how she feels in the third floor hallway," Michael said, "doesn't mean she isn't in touch with her emotions."

How does he do that? How is it that he is able to

magically put into words exactly what I feel, but seem to have so much trouble saying? This, you see, is why I love him. I mean, how could I not?

"Yeah," I said triumphantly.

"Well, you could have said something back to him." Lilly always gets disgruntled when Michael comes to my rescue—especially when he does it while she is attacking me about the lack of honesty in my emotional life. "Instead of just leaving him hanging there."

"And what," I demanded—injudiciously, I now realize—"should I have said to him?"

"How about," Lilly said, "that you love him back?"

WHY? That's all I want to know. WHY was I cursed with a best friend who doesn't understand that there are some things you just don't say in front of EVERYONE IN THE ENTIRE GIFTED AND TALENTED CLASSROOM, INCLUDING HER BROTHER????

The problem is, Lilly has never been embarrassed about anything in her life. She simply does not know the meaning of the word *embarrassment*.

"Look," I said, feeling my cheeks begin to burn. I couldn't lie, of course. How could I lie, considering what I now knew about my nostrils? And okay, Lilly hadn't figured it out yet, but it was only a matter of time. I mean, if *Grandmère* knew . . . "I really and truly value Kenny's companionship," I said, carefully. "But love. I mean, *love*. That is a very big thing. I'm not, I mean, I don't . . ."

I dribbled off pathetically, acutely aware that everyone in the room, most especially Michael, was listening.

"I see," Lilly said, narrowing her eyes. "Fear of commitment."

"I do not fear commitment," I insisted. "I just—"

But Lilly's dark eyes were already shining in eager anticipation. She was getting ready to psychoanalyze me, one of her favorite hobbies, unfortunately.

"Let's examine the situation, shall we?" she said. "I mean, here you've got this guy going around the hallways, screaming about how much he loves you, and you just stare at him like a rat caught in the path of the D train. What do you suppose that means?"

"Have you ever considered," I demanded, "that maybe the reason I didn't tell him I love him back is because I—"

I almost said it. Really. I did. I almost said that I don't love Kenny.

But I couldn't. Because if I'd said that, somehow it would have gotten back to Kenny, and that would be even worse than my breaking up with him. I couldn't do it.

So all I said instead was, "Lilly, you know perfectly well I do not fear commitment. I mean, there are lots of boys I—"

"Oh, yeah?" Lilly seemed to be enjoying herself way more than usual. It was almost as if she was playing to an audience. Which, of course, she was. The audience of her brother and his girlfriend. "Name one."

"One what?"

"Name a boy that you could see yourself committing to for all eternity."

"What do you want, a list?" I asked her.

"A list would be nice," Lilly said.

So I drew up the following list:

GUYS MIA THERMOPOLIS COULD SEE HERSELF COMMITTING TO FOR ALL ETERNITY

1. Wolverine of the *X-men*
2. That *Gladiator* guy
3. Will Smith
4. Tarzan from the Disney cartoon
5. The Beast from *Beauty and the Beast*
6. That hot soldier guy from *Mulan*
7. The guy Brendan Fraser played in *The Mummy*
8. Angel
9. Tom on *Daria*
10. Justin Baxendale

But this list turned out to be no good, because Lilly totally took it and analyzed it, and it works out that half the guys on it are actually cartoon characters; one is a vampire; and one is a mutant who can make spikes shoot out of his knuckles.

In fact, except for Will Smith and Justin Baxendale—the good-looking senior who just transferred from Trinity and who a lot of girls at Albert Einstein High School are already in love with—all the guys I listed are fictional creations. Apparently, the fact that I could list no guy I had a hope of actually getting together with—or who even lives in the third dimension—is indicative of something.

Not, of course, indicative of the fact that the guy I like was actually in the room at the time, sitting next to his new girlfriend, and so I couldn't list him.

Oh, no. Nobody thought of *that*.

No, the lack of actual attainable men on my list was apparently indicative of my unrealistic expectations where men are concerned, and further proof of my inability to commit.

Lilly says if I don't lower my expectations somewhat, I am destined for an unsatisfactory love life.

As if the way things have been going, I've ever expected anything else.

Kenny just tossed me this note:

Mia—I'm sorry about what happened today in the hallway. I understand now that I embarrassed you. Sometimes I forget that even though you are a princess, you are still quite introverted. I promise never to do anything like that again. Can I make it

up to you by taking you to lunch at Big Wong on
Thursday?   —Kenny

I said yes, of course. Not just because I really like
Big Wong's steamed vegetable dumplings, or even
because I don't want people thinking I fear commitment. I didn't even say yes because I suspect that, over
dumplings and hot tea, Kenny is finally going to ask me
to the Nondenominational Winter Dance.

I said yes because in spite of it all, I really do like
Kenny, and I don't want to hurt his feelings.

And I'd feel the same way even if I weren't a
princess, and always had to do the right thing.

HOMEWORK

Algebra: review questions at the end of Chapters
4–7
English: term paper
World Civ: review questions at the end of
Chapters 5–9
G & T: none
French: review questions at the end of Chapters
4–6
Biology: review questions at the end of Chapters
6–8

Tuesday, December 9, 4 p.m.,
in the limo on the way to the Plaza

The following conversation took place between Mr. Gianini and me today after Algebra review:

Mr. G: Mia, is everything all right?

Me: (Surprised) Yes. Why wouldn't it be?

Mr. G: Well, it's just that I thought you'd pretty much grasped the FOIL method, but on today's pop quiz, you got all five problems wrong.

Me: I guess I've sort of had a lot on my mind.

Mr. G: Your trip to Genovia?

Me: Yeah, that, and . . . other things.

Mr. G: Well, if you want to talk about the, um, other things, you know I'm always here for you. And your mother. I know we might seem preoccupied with the baby coming and everything, but you're always number one on our list of priorities. You know that, don't you?

Me: (Mortified) Yes. But there's nothing wrong. Really.

Thank God he doesn't know about my nostrils.

And really, what else *could* I have said? "Mr. G, my boyfriend is a nut case but I can't break up with him on account of finals, and I'm in love with my best friend's brother?"

I highly doubt he'd be able to offer any meaningful advice on any of the above.

I don't believe this. I'm home before *Baywatch Hawaii* starts for the first time in, like, months. Something must be wrong with Grandmère. Although she seemed pretty normal at our lesson today. I mean, for her. Except that she stopped me in the middle of my reciting the Genovian pledge of allegiance (which I have to memorize, of course, for when I am visiting schools in Genovia. I don't want to look like an idiot in front of a bunch of five-year-olds for not knowing it) to ask me what I'd decided to do about Kenny.

It's kind of funny about her taking an interest in my personal life, since she certainly never has before. Well, not very much, anyway.

And she kept on saying stuff about how ingenious it had been of Kenny, sending me those anonymous love letters last October, the ones I thought (well, okay, *hoped*, not really thought) Michael was writing.

I was all, "What was so ingenious about *that*?" to which Grandmère just replied, "Well, you're his girl-friend now, aren't you?"

Which I never really thought about, but I guess she's right.

Anyway, my mom was so surprised to see me home so early, she actually let me be in charge of choosing the takeout (pizza margherita for me. I let her get riga-toni bolognese, even though the sausage in the sauce is probably steeped in nitrates that could harm a developing fetus. Still, it was sort of a special occasion, what with me actually being home for dinner for a change. Even Mr. Gianini got a little wild and had something with porcini mushrooms in it).

I am psyched to be home early, because you wouldn't believe all the studying I have to do, plus I should probably start my term paper, then there's figuring out what I'm going to get people for Christmas and Hannukah, not to mention going over the thank-you speech I have to make to the people of Genovia in my nationally televised (in Genovia, anyway) introduction to the people I will one day rule.

I had really better buckle down and get to work!

Tuesday, December 9, 7:30 p.m.

Okay, so I was taking a study break, and I just realized something. You can learn *a lot* from watching *Baywatch*. Seriously.

I have compiled this list:

THINGS I HAVE LEARNED FROM WATCHING *BAYWATCH*

1. If you are paralyzed from the waist down, you just need to see a kid being attacked by a murderer, and you will be able to get up and save him.
2. If you have bulimia, it is probably because two men love you at the same time. Just tell the two of them you only want to be friends, and your bulimia will go away.
3. It is always easy to get a parking place near the beach.
4. Male lifeguards always put a shirt on when they leave the beach. Female lifeguards don't need to bother.
5. If you meet a beautiful but troubled girl, she is probably either a diamond smuggler or suffering from split personality disorder: Do not accept her invitation to dinner.
6. Dick van Patten, though a senior citizen, can

be surprisingly hard to quell in a fistfight.

7. If people are mysteriously dying in the water, it is probably because a giant electric eel has escaped from a nearby aquarium.

8. A girl who is thinking about abandoning her baby should just leave it on the beach. Chances are, a nice lifeguard will take it home, adopt it, and raise it as his own.

9. It is very easy to outswim a shark.

10. Wild seals make adorable and easily trained pets.

Tuesday, December 9, 8:30 p.m.

I just got an e-mail from Lilly. I'm not the only one who got it, either. Somehow she figured out how to do a mass e-mail to every kid in school.

Well, I shouldn't be surprised, I guess. She *is* a genius. Still, she has clearly developed atrophy of the brain from too much studying, because look what she wrote:

ATTENTION ALL STUDENTS AT ALBERT EINSTEIN HIGH SCHOOL

Stressed from too many exams, term papers, and final projects? Don't just passively accept the oppressive workload handed down to us by the tyrannical administration! A silent walkout has been scheduled for tomorrow. At 10 A.M. exactly, join your fellow students in showing our teachers how we feel about inflexible exam schedules, repressive censorship, and having only one reading day on which to prepare for our finals. Leave your pencils, leave your books, and gather on East 75th Street between Madison and Park (use doors by main administration offices, if possible) for a rally against Principal Gupta and the trustees. Let your voice be heard!

I am so sure. I can't walk out tomorrow at 10 A.M. That's right in the middle of Algebra. Mr. Gianini's feelings will be so hurt if we all just get up and leave.

But if I say I'm not going to take part in it, Lilly will be furious.

But if I do take part in it, my dad will kill me. Not to mention my mom. I mean, we could all get suspended, or something. Or hit by a delivery truck. There are a lot of them on 75th at that time of day.

Why? Why must I be saddled with a best friend who is so clearly a sociopath?

Tuesday, December 9, 8:45 p.m.

I just got the following Instant Message from Michael:

CracKing: Did you just get that whacked-out mass e-mail from my sister?

I replied at once.

FtLouie: Yes.

CracKing: You're not going along with her stupid walkout, are you?

FtLouie: Oh, right. She won't be too mad if I don't, or anything.

CracKing: You don't have to do everything she says, you know, Mia. I mean, you've stood up to her before. Why not now?

Um, because I have enough to worry about right now—for instance, finals; my impending trip to Genovia; and, oh, yeah, the fact that I love you—without adding a fight with my best friend to the list.

But I didn't say that, of course.

FtLouie: I find that the path of least resistance is often the safest one when dealing with your sister.

CracKing: Well, I'm not doing it. Walking out, I mean.

FtLouie: It's different for you. You're her brother. She has to remain on speaking terms with you. You live together.

CracKing: Not for much longer. Thank God.

Oh, right. He's going away to college soon.

Well, not too far away. But about a hundred blocks or so.

FtLouie: That's right. You got accepted to Columbia. Early decision, too. I never did congratulate you. So congratulations.

CracKing: Thanks.

FtLouie: You must be happy that you'll know at least one other person there. Judith Gershner, I mean.

CracKing: Yeah, I guess so. Listen, you're still going to be in town for the Winter Carnival, right? I mean, you're not leaving for Genovia before the 19th are you?

All I could think was, *Why is he asking me this? I mean, he can't be going to ask me to the dance. He must know I'm going with Kenny. I mean, if Kenny ever gets around to asking me, that is. Besides, it isn't as if Michael is available. Isn't he going with Judith? Well? ISN'T HE?*

FtLouie: I'm leaving for Genovia on the 20th.

CracKing: Oh, good. Because you should really stop by the Computer Club's booth at the Carnival, and check out this program I've been working on. I think you'll like it.

I should have known. Michael isn't going to ask me to any dance. Not in this lifetime, anyway. I should have known it was just his stupid computer program he wanted me to see. Who even cares? I suppose dumb army guys will pop out at me, and I'll have to shoot them, or whatever. Judith's idea, I'm sure.

I wanted to write to him, *Don't you have the slightest idea what I'm going through? That the only person with whom I can see myself committing to for all eternity is YOU? Don't you KNOW that by now????*

But instead I wrote:

FtLouie: Can't wait. Well, I have to go. Bye.

Sometimes I completely hate myself.

Wednesday, December 10, 3 a.m.

You're never going to believe this. Something *Grandmère* said is keeping me awake.

Seriously. I was dead asleep—well, as asleep as you can be with a twenty-five pound cat purring on your abdomen—when all of a sudden, I woke up with this totally random phrase going around in my head:

"Well, you're his girlfriend now, aren't you?"

That's what Grandmère said when I asked her what was so ingenious about Kenny's having sent me those anonymous love letters.

And do you know what?

SHE'S RIGHT.

It seems totally bizarre to admit that Grandmère might be right about something, but I think it's true. Kenny's anonymous love letters *did* work. I mean, I *am* his girlfriend now.

So what's to keep me from writing some anonymous love letters to the boy *I* like? I mean, really? Besides the fact that I already have a boyfriend, and the guy I like already has a girlfriend?

I think this is a plan that might have some merit. It needs more work, of course, but hey, desperate measures call for desperate times. Or something like that. Too sleepy to figure it out.

Wednesday, December 10, Homeroom

Okay, I was up all night thinking about it, and I'm pretty sure I've got it figured out. Even as I sit here, my plan is being put into action, thanks to Tina Hakim Baba and a stop at Ho's Deli before school started.

Actually, Ho's didn't really have what I wanted. I wanted a card that was blank inside, with a picture on the front that was sophisticated but not too sexy. But the only blank cards they had at Ho's (that weren't plastered with pictures of kittens) were ones with photos of fruit being dipped into chocolate sauce.

I tried to choose a non-phallic fruit, but even the strawberry I got is kind of sexier than I would have liked. I don't know what's sexy about fruit with chocolate sauce dripping off it, but Tina was like, "Whoa," when she saw it.

Still, she gamely agreed to print my poem on the inside of the card, so Michael won't recognize my handwriting. She even liked my poem, which I came up with at five this morning:

> *Roses are Red*
> *Violets are Blue*
> *You may not know it*
> *But someone loves you.*

Not my best work, I will admit, but it was really hard to come up with something better after only three hours of sleep.

I hesitated somewhat over the use of the L word. I thought maybe I should substitute *like* for *love*. I don't want him to think there's a creepy stalker after him, and all.

But Tina said *love* was absolutely right. Because, as she put it, "It's the truth, isn't it?"

And since it's anonymous, I guess it doesn't matter that I am laying open my soul.

Anyway, Tina goes by Michael's locker right before we have PE, so she's going to slip it to him then.

I can't believe that this is the low I have stooped to. But like Dad once told me, Faint heart never won fair lady.

Wednesday, December 10, Homeroom

Lars just pointed out that I'm not exactly risking anything, seeing as how I didn't sign the card and even went to the extreme of having someone else write out the poem for me (Lars knows all about this, on account of I had to explain to him why we had to go into Ho's at eight fifteen in the morning). He helped pick the card, but I would be happy if that was the extent of his contribution to this particular project. Because he's a man, I cannot imagine his input is at all valuable.

Besides, he's been married like four times, so I highly doubt he knows anything about romance.

Also, he should know by now we're not allowed to talk during Homeroom.

Wednesday, December 10, Algebra, 9:30 a.m.

I just saw Lilly in the hallway. She whispered, "Don't forget! Ten o'clock! Don't let me down!"

Well, the truth is, I did forget. The walkout! The stupid walkout!

And poor Mr. Gianini, standing up there going over Chapter Five, not suspecting a thing. It's not his fault Mrs. Spears didn't like Lilly's term paper topic. Lilly can't just arbitrarily punish all the teachers in school for something one teacher did.

It's already nine thirty-five. What am I going to do?

Lana just leaned back and hissed, "You gonna walk out with your fat friend?"

I take real objection to this. Only in a culture as screwed up as ours, where girls like Christina Aguilera are held up as models of beauty when clearly they are in fact suffering from some sort of malnutrition (scurvy?), would Lilly ever be considered fat. Because Lilly isn't fat. She is just round, like a puppy.

I hate it here.

Wednesday, December 10, Algebra, 9:50 a.m.

Ten minutes until the walkout. I can't take this. I'm getting out.

Wednesday, December 10, 9:55 a.m.

Okay. I'm standing in the hallway next to the fire alarm by the second-floor drinking fountain. I got a hall pass from Mr. G. I told him I had to go to the bathroom.

Lars is with me, of course. I wish he'd stop laughing. He does not seem to realize the seriousness of the situation. Plus Justin Baxendale just walked by with a hall pass of his own, and he gave us this really weird look.

And yeah, I probably do look a little strange, hanging out in the hallway with my bodyguard, who is currently experiencing a fit of the giggles, but still—I do not need to be looked at weirdly by Justin Baxendale.

His eyelashes are really long and dark and they make his eyes look sort of smoky. . . .

OH, MY GOD! I CAN'T BELIEVE I AM WRITING ABOUT JUSTIN BAXENDALE'S EYELASHES AT A TIME LIKE THIS!

I mean, I am in a real bind here:

If I do not walk out with Lilly, I'll lose my best friend.

But if I do walk out with everyone, I will be totally dissing my stepfather.

So I really only have one choice.

Lars just offered to do it for me. But I can't let him. I can't let him take the fall for me if we get caught. I am the princess. I have to do it myself.

I just told him to get ready to run. This is one time being so tall comes in handy. I have a pretty long stride.

Well, here goes.

I don't get why she's so mad. I mean, yeah, if everyone evacuates the building due to a fire alarm going off, it's not the same thing as everyone leaving in protest against the repressive teaching techniques of some of the teachers.

But we're still all standing in the middle of the street in the rain, and nobody has coats on because they wouldn't let us stop at our lockers for fear we'd all be consumed in a fiery conflagration, so we're probably going to get hypothermia from the cold and die.

That's what she wanted, right?

But no. She can't even be happy about that.

"Somebody ratted us out!" she keeps yelling. "Somebody told! Why else would they schedule a fire drill for exactly the same time as my walkout? I'm telling you, these bureaucrats will stop at nothing to keep us from speaking out against them. Nothing! They'll even make us stand out in freezing drizzle, hoping to weaken our immune systems so we'll no longer have the strength to fight them. Well, I for one refuse to catch cold! I refuse to succumb to their petty abuses!"

I suggested to Lilly that she write her term paper on the suffragettes, because they, like us, had to put up with numerous indignities in their battle for equal rights.

Lilly, however, told me not to be facile.

God, being best friends with a genius is hard.

I can't tell if Michael got the note or not!!!!

Worse, stupid Judith Gershner is here AGAIN. Why can't she stay in her own class? Why is she always hanging around ours? We were all getting along perfectly well until *she* came along.

My life is pathetic.

I thought about going across the hall to the teachers' lounge and asking Mrs. Hill a question about something—like why she had the custodians remove the door to the supply closet so we can't lock Boris in there anymore—so she'd maybe look over and NOTICE that there's a girl in our classroom who is *not* supposed to be there.

But I couldn't bring myself to do it, because of Michael. I mean, Michael obviously *wants* Judith here, or else he'd tell her to go away.

RIGHT?????

Anyway, with Michael so busy and all with Miss Gershner, I guess I am on my own with the whole Algebra review thing.

That's all right. I'm completely fine with that. I can study on my own just fine. Watch:

A, B, C = disjoint partition of universal set
Collection of non-empty subsets of U that are pairwise disjoint and whose union is equal to the set of U

I get that. I totally get what that means. Who needs Michael's help? Not me. I am totally cool with the collection of non-empty subsets.

TOTALLY COOL WITH IT.

> *Oh, Michael*
> *You have made my heart*
> *a disjoint partition.*
>
> *Why can't you see*
> *that we were meant to be*
> *a universal set?*
>
> *Instead, you have turned my soul*
> *into a collection*
> *of non-empty subsets.*
>
> *I cannot believe*
> *that our love was meant to be*
> *pairwise disjoint.*
>
> *But rather*
> *a union—*
> *equal to the set of*
> *U and me.*

You know what else I just realized? That if this thing works—you know, if I do manage to get Michael away from Judith Gershner, and I break up with Kenny, and I end up, you know, in a potentially romantic situation with Lilly's brother—I will not know what to do.

Seriously.

Take kissing, for instance. I have only ever kissed one person before, and that's Kenny. I cannot believe that what Kenny and I did really encompassed the whole of the kissing experience, because it certainly wasn't as fun as people always make it look on TV.

This is a very disturbing thought, and has led me to an equally disturbing conclusion: I know very little about kissing.

In fact, it seems to me that if I am going to be doing any kissing with anybody, I should get some advice beforehand. From a kissing expert, I mean.

Which is why I am consulting Tina Hakim Baba. She may not be allowed to wear makeup to school, but she has been kissing Dave Farouq El-Abar—who goes to Trinity—for close to three months now, *and* liking it, so I consider her an expert on the subject.

I am enclosing the results of this highly scientific document for future reference.

Tina—

I need to know about kissing. Can you please answer
each of the following questions IN DETAIL????
And DO NOT show this to anyone!!!! DO NOT
lose this paper!!!! —Mia

1. Can a boy tell if the person he is with is
inexperienced? How does an inexperienced kisser
kiss (so I can avoid that)?

> *The guy may sense a feeling of nervousness coming
> from you, or that you are uneasy, but everyone is
> nervous when they are kissing someone new. It's
> natural! But kissing is easy to catch on to—believe
> me! An inexperienced kisser might break away too
> soon because he or she is scared or whatever. But
> that is normal. It's SUPPOSED to be weird.
> That's what makes it fun.*

2. Is there such a thing as a great kisser? If so, what
are the qualifications? (So I know what to practice.)

> *Yes, there is such a thing as a great kisser. A great
> kisser is always affectionate and gentle and patient and
> not demanding.*

3. How much pressure do you exert on his lips? I
mean, do you push, or like in a handshake, are you

just supposed to be firm? Or are you just supposed to stand there and let him do all the work?

> *If you want a gentle kiss (a caring one) don't apply too much pressure (this is also true if he is wearing braces—you don't want to cause any lacerations). If you give a guy a "harsh" kiss (too much pressure), he might think you are desperate or that you want to go further than you probably do.*
>
> *Of course you aren't supposed to just stand there and let him do all the work: kiss him back! But always kiss him the way YOU want to be kissed. That is how guys learn. If we didn't show them how to do everything, we'd never get anywhere!*

4. How do you know when it's time to stop?

> *Stop when he stops, or when you feel like you've had enough, or don't want to go any further. Just gently (so you don't freak him out) move your head back, or if the moment is right, you can change the kiss into a hug, then step back.*

5. If you are in love with him, is it still gross?

> *Of course not! Kissing is never gross!*
>
> *Well, okay, I guess I could see that maybe with Kenny, it might be. It is always better with*

someone you actually like.

Of course, even with someone you really like, sometimes kissing can be gross. Once Dave licked me on the chin, and I was all, Get away. But I think that was by accident (the licking).

6. If he is in love with you, does he even care if you are bad? (Define bad kisser. See above.)

If the guy likes/loves you, he won't care if you are a good kisser or not. In fact, even if you are a bad kisser, he will probably think you are a good one. And vice versa. He should like you for what you are—not how you kiss.

DEFINITION OF BAD KISSER: A bad kisser is someone who gets your face all wet, slobbers on you, sticks his tongue in when you're not ready, has bad breath, OR sometimes there can be kissers whose tongues are all dry and prickly like a cactus but I have never experienced one of those, just heard about them.

7. When do you know if it's time to open your mouth (thus turning it into a French)?

You will probably feel his tongue touch your lips. If you want to pursue the idea, open your lips a little. If not, keep them closed.

Coming au demain–Chapter II: How to French!!!!

HOMEWORK

Algebra: review questions at the end of Chapters 8–10
English: English Journal: Books I Have Read
World Civ: review questions at the end of Chapters 10–12
G & T: none
French: review questions at the end of Chapters 7–9
Biology: review questions at the end of Chapters 9–12

I am so tired I can hardly write. Grandmère made me try on every single dress in Sebastiano's showroom. You wouldn't believe the number of dresses I've had on today. Short ones, long ones, straight-skirted ones, poufy-skirted ones, white ones, pink ones, blue ones, and even a lime-green one (which Sebastiano declared brought out the 'col' in my cheeks).

The purpose of all this dress-trying-on business was to choose one to wear on Christmas Eve, during my first official televised speech to the Genovian people. I have to look regal, but not too regal. Beautiful, but not too beautiful. Sophisticated, but not too sophisticated.

I tell you, it was a nightmare of hollow-cheeked women in white (the new black) buttoning and zipping and snapping me in and out of dresses. Now I know how all those supermodels must feel. No wonder they do so many drugs.

Actually, it *was* kind of hard to choose my dress for my first big televised event, because surprisingly, Sebastiano turned out to be a pretty good designer. There were several dresses I actually wouldn't be embarrassed to be caught dead in.

Oops. Slip of the tongue. I wonder, though, if Sebastiano really does want to kill me. He seems to like being a fashion designer, which he couldn't do if he were prince of Genovia: He'd be too busy turning bills into law and stuff like that.

Still, you can tell he'd totally enjoy wearing a crown. Not that, as ruler of Genovia, he'd ever get to do this. I've never seen my dad in a crown. Just suits. And shorts when he plays racquetball with other world leaders.

Ew, I wonder if I will have to learn to play racquetball.

But if Sebastiano became prince of Genovia, he would totally wear a crown all the time. He told me nothing brings out the sparkles in someone's eyes like pear-shaped diamonds. He prefers Tiffany's. Or as he calls it, Tiff's.

Since we were getting so chummy and all, I told Sebastiano about the Nondenominational Winter Dance, and how I have nothing to wear to it. Sebastiano seemed disappointed when he learned I would not be wearing a tiara to my school dance, but he got over it and started asking me all these questions about the event. Like "Who do you go with?" and "What he look like?" and stuff like that.

I don't know what it was, but I found myself actually telling Sebastiano all about my love life. It was so weird. I totally didn't want to, but it all just started spilling out. Thank God Grandmère wasn't there. . . . she'd gone off in search of more cigarettes, and to have her sidecar refreshed.

I told Sebastiano all about Kenny and how he loves me but I don't love him, and how I actually like someone else, but he doesn't know I'm alive.

Sebastiano is actually quite a good listener. I don't know how much, if anything, he understood of what I said, but he didn't take his eyes off my reflection as I talked, and when I was done, he looked me up and down in the mirror, and just said one thing: "This boy you like. How you know he no like you back?"

"Because," I said. "He likes this other girl."

Sebastiano made an impatient motion with his hands. The gesture was made more dramatic by the fact that he was wearing sleeves with these big frilly lace cuffs.

"No, no, no, no, no," he said. "He help you with your Al home. He like you, or he no do that. Why he do that, if he no like you?"

I took "He help you with your Al home" to mean "He helps you with your Algebra homework." I thought for a minute about why Michael had always been so willing to do that. Help me with my Algebra, I mean. I guess just because I am his sister's best friend, and he isn't the type of person who can sit around and watch his sister's best friend flunk out of high school without, you know, at least trying to do something about it.

While I was thinking about that, I couldn't help remembering how Michael's knees, beneath our desks, sometimes brush against mine as he's telling me about integers. Or how sometimes he leans so close to correct something I've written wrong that I can smell the nice, clean scent of his soap. Or how sometimes, like when I do my Lana Weinberger imitation or whatever, he throws back his head and laughs.

Michael's lips look extra nice when he is smiling.

"Tell Sebastiano," Sebastiano urged me. "Tell Sebastiano why this boy help you, if he no like you."

I sighed. "Because I'm his little sister's best friend," I said sadly. Really, could there *be* anything more humiliating? I mean, clearly Michael has never been impressed with my keen intellect or ravishing good looks, given my low grade-point average and of course my gigantism.

Sebastiano tugged on my sleeve and went, "You no worry. I make dress for dance, this boy, he no think of you as little sister's best friend."

Yeah. Sure. Whatever. Why must all my relatives be so weird?

Anyway, we picked out what I'm going to wear on Genovian national TV during my introduction. It's this white taffeta job with a huge poufy skirt and this light blue sash (the royal colors are blue and white). But Sebastiano had one of his assistants take photos of me in all the dresses, so I can see how I looked in them and then decide. I thought this was fairly professional for a guy who calls breakfast "breck."

But all that isn't what I want to write about. I'm so tired, I hardly know what I'm doing. What I want to write about is what happened today after Algebra review.

Which was that Mr. Gianini, after everyone but me had left, went, "Mia, I heard a rumor that there was supposed to have been some kind of student walkout today. Had you heard that?"

Me:	(freezing in my seat) Um, no.
Mr. Gianini:	Oh. So you wouldn't know then if somebody—maybe in protest of the protest—threw the second-floor fire alarm? The one by the drinking fountain?
Me:	(wishing Lars would stop coughing suggestively) Um, no.
Mr. Gianini:	That's what I thought. Because you know the penalty for pulling one of the fire alarms—when there is, in fact, no sign of a fire—is expulsion.
Me:	Oh, yes. I know that.
Mr. Gianini:	I thought you might have seen who did it, since I believe I gave you a hall pass shortly before the alarm went off.
Me:	Oh, no. I didn't see anybody.

Except Justin Baxendale, and his smoky eyelashes.
But I didn't say that.

Mr. Gianini: I didn't think so. Oh, well. If you ever
                hear who did it, maybe you could tell
                her from me never to do it again.
Me: Um. Okay.
Mr. Gianini: And tell her thanks from me, too. The
                last thing we need right now, with
                tensions running so high over finals, is
                a student walkout. (Mr. Gianini picked
                up his briefcase and jacket.) See you at
                home.

Then he winked at me. WINKED at me, like he
knew I was the one who'd done it. But he couldn't
know. I mean, he doesn't know about my nostrils
(which were fully flaring the whole time; I could *feel*
them!) Right? RIGHT????

Thursday, December 11, Homeroom

Lilly is going to drive me crazy.

Seriously. Like it's not enough I have finals and my introduction to Genovia and my love life and everything to worry about. I have to listen to Lilly complain about how the administration of Albert Einstein High is out to get her. The whole way to school this morning she just droned on and on about how it's all a plot to silence her because she once complained about the Coke machine outside the gym. Apparently the Coke machine is indicative of the administration's efforts to turn us all into mindless soda-drinking, Gap-wearing clones, in Lilly's opinion.

If you ask me, this isn't really about Coke, or the attempts by the school's administration to turn us into mindless pod-people. It's really just because Lilly's still mad she can't use a chapter of the book she's writing on the high-school experience as her term paper.

I reminded Lilly if she doesn't submit a new topic, she's going to get an F as her nine-week grade. Factored in with her A for the last nine weeks, that's only like a C, which will significantly lower her grade-point average, and put her chances of getting into Berkeley, which is her first-choice school, at risk. She may be forced to fall back on her safety school, Brown, which I know would be quite a blow.

She didn't even listen to me. She says she's having

an organizational meeting of this new group (of which she is president) Students Against the Corporatization of Albert Einstein High School (SACAEHS) on Saturday, and I have to come, because I am the group's secretary. Don't ask me how *that* happened. Lilly says I write everything down anyway, so it shouldn't be any trouble for me.

I wish Michael had been there to protect me from his sister, but like he has every day this week, he took the subway to school early so he could work on his project for the Winter Carnival.

I wouldn't doubt Judith Gershner has been showing up to school on the early side, too, this week.

Speaking of whom, I picked up another greeting card, this one from the Plaza gift shop on the way to Sebastiano's showroom last night. It's a lot better than that stupid one with the strawberry. This one has a picture of a lady holding a finger to her lips. Inside, it says, *Shhhh . . .*

Under that, I am having Tina write:

> *Roses are red*
> *But cherries are redder*
> *Maybe she can clone fruit flies*
> *But I like you better.*

What I meant was that I like him more than Judith Gershner does, but I'm not really sure that comes through in the poem. Tina says it does, but Tina thinks I should have used love instead of like, so who knows if her opinion is of any value? This is a poem clearly calling for a like and not a love.

I should know. I write enough of them.

Poems, I mean.

This semester, we have read several novels, including *To Kill a Mockingbird*, *Huckleberry Finn*, and *The Scarlet Letter*. In your English journal, please record your feelings about the books we have read, and books in general. What have been your most meaningful experiences as a reader? Your favorite books? Your least favorite?

Please utilize <u>transitive</u> verbs.

BOOKS I HAVE READ,
AND WHAT THEY MEANT TO ME
by Mia Thermopolis

Books that were good:

1. *Jaws*—I bet you didn't know that in the book version of this, Richard Dreyfuss and Roy Scheider's wife have sex. But they do.
2. *The Catcher in the Rye*—This is totally good. It has lots of bad words.
3. *To Kill a Mockingbird*—This is an excellent book. They should do a movie version of this with Mel Gibson as Atticus, and he should blow Mr. Ewell away with a flame thrower at the end.
4. *A Wrinkle in Time*—Only we never find out the most important thing: whether or not Meg has

breasts. I'm thinking she probably did, considering the fact that she already had the glasses and braces. I mean, all of that, and flat-chested, too? God wouldn't be so cruel.

5. *Emanuelle*—In the eighth grade, my best friend and I found this book on top of a trash can on East Third Street. We took turns reading it out loud. It was very, very good. At least the parts I remember. My mom caught us reading it and took it away before we'd gotten a chance to finish it.

Books that sucked*

1. *The Scarlet Letter*—You know what would have been cool? If there had been a rift in the space-time continuum, and one of those Euro-trash terrorists Bruce Willis is always chasing in the Die Hard movies dropped a nuclear bomb on the town where Arthur Dimmesdale and all those losers lived, and blew it sky high. That's about the only thing I can think of that would have made this book even remotely interesting.

2. *Our Town*—Okay, this is a play and not a book, but they still made us read it, and all I have to say about it is that basically, you find out when you die that nobody cared about you and we're all alone forever, the end. Okay! Thanks for that! I feel much better now!

3. *The Mill on the Floss*—I don't want to give anything

away here, but midway through the book, just when things were going good and there were all these hot romances (not as hot as in *Emanuelle*, though, so don't get your hopes up) someone very crucial to the plot DIES, which if you ask me is just a cop-out so the author could make her deadline on time.

4. *Anne of Green Gables*—All that blah-blah-blah about imagination. I tried to imagine some car chases or explosions that would actually make this book good, but I must be like all of Anne's drippy unimaginative friends, because I couldn't.

5. *Little House on the Prairie*—Little yawn on the big snore. I have all ninety-seven thousand of these books, because people kept on giving them to me when I was little, and all I have to say is if Half Pint had lived in Manhattan, she'd have gotten her you-know-what-kicked from here to Avenue D.

---

* Mrs. Spears, I believe the word *sucked* is transitive in this instance.

No PE today!

Instead there is an assembly.

And it's not because there's a sporting event they want us all to show our support for. No! This was no pep rally. There wasn't a cheerleader in sight. Well, okay, there were cheerleaders in sight, but they weren't in uniform or anything. They were sitting in the bleachers with the rest of us. Well, not really with the rest of us, since they were in the best seats, the ones in the middle, all jostling to see who could sit next to Justin Baxendale, who has apparently ousted Josh Richter as hottest guy in school, but whatever.

No. Instead, it appears that there has been a major disciplinary infraction at Albert Einstein High School. An act of random vandalism that has shaken the administration's faith in us. Which was why they called an assembly, so that they could better convey their feelings of—as Lilly just whispered in my ear—disillusionment and betrayal.

And what was this act that has Principal Gupta and the trustees so up in arms?

Why, someone pulled a fire alarm yesterday, that's what.

Oops.

I have to say, I have never done anything really bad before—well, I dropped an eggplant out a sixteenth floor window a couple of months ago, but no one got hurt or anything—but there really is something sort of thrilling about it. I mean, I would never want to do anything *too* bad, like anything where someone might get hurt.

But I have to say, it is immensely gratifying to have all these people coming up to the microphone and decrying my behavior.

I probably wouldn't feel so good about it if I'd gotten caught, though.

I am being urged to come forward and turn myself in even as I write this. Apparently, the guilt for my action is going to hound me well past my teen years, possibly even into my twenties and beyond.

Okay, can I just tell you how much I'm NOT going to think about high school when I am in my twenties? I am going to be way too busy working with Greenpeace to save the whales to worry about some stupid fire alarm I pulled in the ninth grade.

The administration is offering a reward for information leading to the identity of the perpetrator of this heinous crime. A reward! You know what the reward is? A free movie pass to the Sony Imax theater. That's all I'm worth! A movie pass!

The only person who could possibly turn me in isn't even paying attention to the assembly. I can see Justin Baxendale has got a Gameboy out, and is playing it with the sound off, while Lana and her fellow cheer cronies look over his broad shoulders, probably panting so hard they're fogging up the screen.

I guess Justin hasn't put two and two together yet. You know, about seeing me in the hallway just before that fire alarm went off. With any luck, he never will.

Mr. Gianini, though. That's another story. I see him over there, talking to Mrs. Hill. He has obviously not told anyone that he suspects me.

Maybe he doesn't suspect me. Maybe he thinks Lilly did it, and I know about it. That could be. I can tell Lilly really wishes she'd done it, because she keeps on muttering under her breath about how, when she finds out who did it, she's going to kill that person, etc.

She's just jealous, of course. That's because now it seems like some kind of political statement, instead of what it actually was: a way to prevent a political statement.

Principal Gupta is looking at us very sternly. She says that it is always natural to want to burn off a little steam right before finals, but that she hopes we will choose positive channels for this, such as the penny drive the Community Outreach Club is holding in order to benefit the victims of Tropical Storm Fred, which flooded several suburban New Jersey neighborhoods last November.

Ha! As if contributing to a stupid penny drive can ever give anybody the same kind of thrill as committing a completely random act of civil disobedience.

LILLY MOSCOVITZ'S LIST OF THE
TOP TEN BEST MOVIES OF ALL TIME
(with commentary by Mia Thermopolis)

Say Anything: Kick-boxing iconoclast Lloyd Dobler,
as played by John When-is-He-Going-to-Run-
for-President-So-We-Can-Have-Someone-Cute-in-the-
Oval-Office Cusack, goes after the class brain (Ione
Skye), who soon learns what we all know: Lloyd is
every girl's dream date. He understands us. He longs
to protect us from broken glass in the parking lot of the
local Seven Eleven. Need we say more? (*This movie
also contains classic song,* Joe Lies.)

Reckless: Rebel from wrong side of tracks (Aidan
Quinn) goes after straight-arrow cheerleader (Daryl
Hannah). A classic example of teens struggling to
break the yoke of parental expectation. *(Plus you get
to see Aidan Quinn's you-know-what!)*

Desperately Seeking Susan: Bored suburban
housewife finds man of her dreams in East Village.
An Eighties manifesto about female empowerment.
Also starring Madonna and that lady who played
Roseanne's sister Jackie. (*Also starring Aidan Quinn
as the East Village hottie, only you don't really get to
see his you-know-what in this one. But you do get to
see his butt!*)

Ladyhawke: Star-crossed lovers are caught in an evil spell that only Matthew Broderick can help them break. Rutger Hauer makes a powerful Navarre, a knight who lives only to exact vengeance upon the man who wronged his fair Isabeau, played by Michelle Pfeiffer. An elegant and moving love story. (*But what is with Matthew Broderick's hair?*)

Dirty Dancing: Spoiled teenage Baby learns a lot more than the cha-cha from long-haired summer resort dance instructor Johnny. A classic tale of coming-of-age in the Catskills, with important messages about the class system in America. (*Only you don't get to see anyone's butt.*)

Flashdance: A welder by day and an exotic dancer by night, Jennifer Beals's Alex is a feminist in a thong, the Elizabeth Cady Stanton of the lap dance, who longs to audition for the Pittsburgh ballet. (*But first she sleeps with her totally hot boss Michael Nouri and throws a big rock through his window!*)

The Cutting Edge: Former hockey stud D. B. Sweeney is paired with figure skater and prissy rich girl Moira Kelly in an unlikely quest for Olympic gold. Interesting for its strategic build-up of sexual tension through pairs skating. (*Toe-pick. Toooooooe-pick.*)

Some Kind of Wonderful: Victory of tomboy Mary Stuart Masterson over prissy Lea Thompson for the heart of Eric Stolz. As usual, keen insight by John Hughes into the teen psyche/social structure. (*Last movie in which Eric Stolz was actually cute.*)

Reality Bites: Who will indie filmmaker Winona Ryder choose, smart aleck slacker Ethan Hawke, or clean-cut go-getter Ben Stiller? (*Isn't it obvious?*)

Footloose: Out-of-towner flaunts small town's anti-dancing laws. Starring Kevin Bacon, who saves Lori Singer from her abusive hick boyfriend. Most notable for scene at the PTA meeting in which Kevin Bacon's character reveals he has actually done homework, as illustrated by his quoting from several Biblical passages which support dancing. (*In the movies* Wild Things *and* Hollow Man *you get to see Kevin Bacon's you-know-what.*)

Today was my lunch with Kenny at Big Wong.

I really don't have anything to say about it, except that he didn't ask me to the Nondenominational Winter Dance. Not only that, but it appears that Kenny's passion for me has ebbed significantly since it hit its zenith on Tuesday.

I of course was beginning to suspect this, since he's stopped calling me after school, and I haven't had one Instant Message from him since before the great Ice-Skating Debacle. He says it's because he's so busy studying for finals and all, but I suspect something else:

He knows. He knows about Michael.

I mean, come on. How can he not?

Well, okay, maybe he doesn't know about Michael *specifically,* but Kenny must know *generally* that he is not the one who lights my fire.

If I had a fire, that is.

No, Kenny is just being nice.

Which I appreciate, and all, but I just wish he'd come out and say it. All of this kindness, this solicitousness, it's just making me feel worse. I mean, how could I? Really? How could I have ever agreed to be Kenny's girlfriend, knowing full well I liked someone else? By rights, Kenny should go to *Majesty* magazine and spill all. "Royal Betrayal," they could call it. I totally would understand it, if he did.

But he won't. Because he's too nice.

Instead, he ordered steamed vegetable dumplings for me, and pork buns for him (one encouraging sign that Kenny might not love me as much as he used to insist: he's eating meat again) and talked about Bio and what had happened at assembly (I didn't tell him it was me who pulled the alarm, and he didn't ask me, so there was no need to shield my nostrils). He mentioned again how sorry he was about my tongue, and asked how I was doing in Algebra, and offered to come over and tutor me if I wanted (Kenny tested out of freshman Algebra), even though of course I live with an Algebra teacher. Still, you could tell he meant to be nice.

Which just makes me feel worse. Because of what I'm going to have to do after finals and all.

But he didn't ask me to the dance.

I don't know if this means we aren't going, or if it means he considers the fact we are going a given.

I swear, I do not understand boys at all.

As if lunch wasn't bad enough, G and T isn't too great, either. No, Judith Gershner isn't here . . . but neither is Michael. The guy is AWOL. Nobody knows where he is. Lilly had to tell Mrs. Hill, when she took attendance, that her brother was in the bathroom.

I wonder where he really is. Lilly says that since he started writing this new program that the Computer Club will be unveiling at the Winter Carnival, she's hardly seen him.

Which is no real change, since Michael hardly comes out of his room anyway, but still. You'd think he'd come home once in a while to study.

But I guess, seeing as how he already got into his first-choice college, his grades don't really matter anymore.

Besides, like Lilly, Michael is a genius. What does he need to study for?

Unlike the rest of us.

I wish they'd put the door back on the supply closet. It is extremely hard to concentrate with Boris scraping away on his violin in there. Lilly says this is just another tactic by the trustees to weaken our resistance, so we will remain the mindless drones they are trying to make us, but I think it's just on account of that time we all forgot to let him out, and he was stuck in there until the night custodian heard his anguished pleas to be released.

Which is Lilly's fault, if you think about it. I mean, she's his girlfriend. She should really take better care of him.

HOMEWORK

Algebra: practice test
English: term paper
World Civ: practice test
G & T: none
French: l'examen pratique
Biology: practice test

Grandmère is seriously out of control. Tonight she started quizzing me on the names and responsibilities of all of my dad's cabinet ministers. Not only do I have to know exactly what they do, but also their marital status and the names and ages of their kids, if any. These are the kids I am supposedly going to have to hang out with while celebrating Christmas at the palace. I am figuring they will probably hate me as much as, if not more than, Mr. Gianini's niece and nephew hated me at Thanksgiving.

All of my holidays from now on are apparently going to be spent in the company of kids who hate me.

You know, I would just like to say that it is totally not my fault I am a princess. They have no right to hate me so much. I have done everything I could to maintain a normal life in spite of my royal status. I have totally turned down opportunities to be on the covers of *CosmoGirl*, *Teen People*, *Seventeen*, *YM*, and *Girl's Life*. I have refused invitations to go on *TRL* and introduce the number-one video in the country, and when the mayor asked if I wanted to be the one to press the button that drops the ball in Times Square on New Year's Eve, I said no (aside from the fact I am going to be in Genovia for New Year's, I oppose the mayor's mosquito spraying campaign, as runoff from the pesticides used to kill the mosquitos that may be carrying the West Nile virus has infected the local horseshoe crab population. A compound in the blood of horseshoe crabs, which nest all along the eastern seaboard, is used to test the purity of every drug and vaccine administered in the U.S. The crabs are routinely gathered, drained of a third of their blood, then re-released into the sea . . . a sea which is now killing them as well as many other arthropods, such as lobsters, thanks to the amount of pesticide in it).

Anyway, I am just saying, all the kids who hate me should just chill, because I have never once sought the spotlight I have been thrust into. I've never even called my own press conference.

But I digress.

So Sebastiano was there, drinking aperitifs and listening as I rattled off name after name (Grandmère has made flashcards out of the pictures of the cabinet ministers—kind of like those bubble gum cards you can get of the Backstreet Boys, only the cabinet ministers don't wear as much leather). I was kind of thinking maybe I was wrong about Sebastiano's commitment to fashion, and that maybe Sebastiano was there to try and pick up some pointers for after he's thrust me into the path of an oncoming limo or whatever.

But when Grandmère paused to take a phone call from her old friend General Pinochet, Sebastiano started asking me all these questions about clothes, in particular what clothes my friends and I like to wear.

What were my feelings, he wanted to know, on velvet stretch pants? Spandex tube tops? Sequins?

I told him all of that sounded, you know, okay for Halloween or Jersey City, but that generally in my day-to-day life I prefer cotton. He looked saddened by this, so I told him that I really felt orange was going to be the next pink, and that perked him right up, and he wrote a bunch of stuff down in this notebook he carries around. Kind of like I do, now that I think about it.

When Grandmère got off the phone, I informed her—quite diplomatically, I might add—that, considering how much progress we'd made in the past three months, I felt more than prepared for my impending introduction to the people of Genovia, and that I did not feel it would be necessary to have lessons next week, as I have FIVE finals to prepare for.

But Grandmère got totally huffy about it! She was all, "Where did you get the idea that your academic education is more important than your royal training? Your father, I suppose. With him, it's always education, education, education. He doesn't realize that education is nowhere near as important as deportment."

"Grandmère," I said. "I need an education if I'm going to run Genovia properly." Especially if I'm going to convert the palace into a giant animal shelter—something I'm not going to be able to do until Grandmère is dead, so I see no point in mentioning it to her now . . . or ever, for that matter.

Grandmère said some swear words in French, which wasn't very dowager-princessy of her, if you ask me. Thankfully right then my dad walked in, looking for his Genovian Air Force medal, since he had a state dinner to go to over at the embassy. I told him about my finals and how I really needed time off from princess stuff to study, and he was all, "Yes, of course."

When Grandmère protested, he just went, "For God's sake, if she hasn't got it by now, she never will."

Grandmère pressed her lips together and didn't say anything more after that. Sebastiano used the opportunity to ask me about my feelings on rayon. I told him I didn't have any.

For once, I was telling the truth.

HERE'S WHAT I HAVE TO DO:

1. Stop thinking about Michael, especially when I should be studying.
2. Stop telling Grandmère anything about my personal life.
3. Start acting more:
   A. Mature
   B. Responsible
   C. Regal
4. Stop biting my fingernails.
5. Write down everything Mom and Mr. G need to know about how to take care of Fat Louie while I'm gone.
6. CHRISTMAS/HANNUKAH PRESENTS!
7. Stop watching *Baywatch* when I should be studying.
8. Stop playing Pod-Racer when I should be studying.
9. Stop listening to music when I should be studying.
10. Break up with Kenny.

Well, I guess it's official now:

I, Mia Thermopolis, am a juvenile delinquent.

Seriously. That fire alarm I pulled was only the beginning, it appears.

I really don't know what's come over me lately. It's like the closer I get to actually going to Genovia and performing my first official duties as its princess, the less like a princess I act.

I wonder if I'll be expelled.

If I am, it is totally unfair. Lana started it. I was sitting there in Algebra, listening to Mr. G go on about the Cartesian plane, when suddenly Lana turns around in her seat and slaps a copy of *USA Today* down in front of me. There is a headline screaming:

TODAY'S POLL

Most Popular Young Royal

Fifty-seven percent of readers say that **Prince William of England** is their favorite young royal, with Will's little brother **Harry** coming in at 28 percent. America's own royal, **Princess Mia Renaldo of Genovia**, comes in third, with 13 percent of the votes, and Prince Andrew and

Sarah Ferguson's daughters, **Beatrice** and **Eugenie**, round out the votes with 1 percent each.

The reasons given for Princess Mia's third-place finish? "Not outgoing" is the most common answer. Ironically, Princess Mia is perceived as being as shy as Princess Diana—the mother of William and Harry—when she first stepped into the harsh glare of the media spotlight.

Princess Mia, who only recently learned she was heir to the throne of Genovia, a small principality located on the Cote d'Azur, is expected to make her first official trip to that country next week. A representative for the princess describes her as looking forward to her visit with "eager anticipation." The princess will continue her education in America, and will reside in Genovia only during the summer months.

I read the stupid article and then passed the paper back to Lana.

"So?" I whispered to her.

"So," Lana whispered. "I wonder how popular you'd be—especially with the people of Genovia—if they found out their future ruler goes around pulling fire alarms when there isn't any fire."

She was only guessing, of course. She couldn't have seen me. Unless . . .

Unless maybe Justin Baxendale did figure it out! You know, seeing me in the hallway like that, just before the alarm went off—and he mentioned it to Lana. . . .

No. Not possible. I am so far out of the sphere of Justin Baxendale's consciousness as to be nonexistent to him. He didn't tell Lana anything. Lana, like Mr. G, obviously thinks it's a little coincidental that on that fateful Wednesday, the fire alarm went off about two minutes after I'd disappeared from class with the pass to the bathroom.

But even so. Even though she could only have been guessing, it seemed to me like she knew, like she was going to make sure I never heard the end of it.

I really don't know what came over me. I don't know if it was

A. The stress of finals
B. My impending trip to Genovia
C. This thing with Kenny
D. The fact that I'm in love with this guy who is going out with a human fruit fly
E. The fact that my mother is going to give birth to my Algebra teacher's baby

F. The fact that Lana has been persecuting me practically my whole life and pretty much getting away with it, or

G. All of the above.

Whatever the reason, I snapped. Just snapped. Suddenly, I found myself reaching for Lana's cell phone, which was lying on her desktop beside her calculator.

And then the next thing I knew, I had put the tiny little pink thing on the floor, and crushed it into a lot of pieces beneath the heel of my size-ten combat boot.

I guess I can't really blame Mr. G for sending me to the principal's office.

Still, you would expect a little sympathy from your own stepfather.

Uh-oh. Here comes Principal Gupta.

Well, that's it then. I'm suspended.

Suspended. I can't believe it. ME! Mia Thermopolis! What is happening to me? I used to be such a good kid!

And okay, it's just for one day, but still. It's going on my permanent record! What are the Genovian cabinet ministers going to say?

I am turning into Courtney Love.

And yeah, it's not like I'm not going to get into college because I was suspended for one day in the first semester of my freshman year, but how totally embarrassing! Principal Gupta treated me like I was some kind of *criminal* or something.

And you know what they say: Treat a person like a criminal, and pretty soon, she'll end up like one. At least I think that's what they say. The way things are going, I wouldn't be surprised if pretty soon I start wearing ripped-up fishnet stockings and dying my hair black. Maybe I'll even start smoking and get my ears double pierced or something. And then they'll make a TV movie about me, and call it *Royal Scandal*. It will show me going up to Prince William and saying, "Who's the most popular young royal now, huh, punk?" and then headbutting him or something.

Except I practically fainted the first time I got my

ears pierced, and smoking is really bad for you, and I always thought it must hurt to headbutt someone.

I guess I don't have the makings of a juvenile delinquent after all.

My dad doesn't think so, either. He's all ready to set the royal Genovian lawyers on Principal Gupta. The only problem, of course, is that I won't tell him—or anybody else, for that matter—what Lana said to make me assault her cell phone. It's kind of hard to prove the attack was provoked if the attacker won't say what the provocation was. My dad pleaded with me for a while when he came to pick me up from school, after having received The Call from Principal Gupta. But when I wouldn't tell him what he wanted, and Lars just looked carefully blank, my dad just went, "Fine," and his mouth got all scrunchy like it does when Grandmère has one too many sidecars and starts calling him Papa Cueball.

But how can I tell him what Lana said? If I do that, then everyone will know I'm guilty of not just one crime, but two!

Anyway, now I'm home, watching the Lifetime channel with my mother. She hasn't been doing much painting at her studio since she got pregnant. This is on account of her being exhausted. It's quite hard to paint lying down, she's discovered. So instead she has been doing a lot of sketching from bed, mostly line drawings of Fat Louie, who seems to enjoy having someone home all day with him. He sits for hours on her bed, watching the pigeons on the fire escape outside her window.

But since I'm home today, Mom did some drawings of me. I think she is making my mouth too big, but I'm not saying anything, as Mr. Gianini and I have discovered it's better not to upset my mother in her current hormonal state. Even the slightest criticism—like asking her why she left the phone bill in the vegetable crisper—can lead to an hour-long crying jag.

While she sketched me, I watched a very excellent movie called *Mother, May I Sleep With Danger?* starring Tori Spelling, of *Beverly Hills 90210* fame, as a girl who has an abusive boyfriend. I really don't get why any girl would stay with a guy who hits her, but my mom says it's all about self-esteem and your relationship with your father. Except that my mom doesn't have that great a relationship with Papaw, and if any guy ever tried to slug her, you can bet she'd put him in the hospital, so go figure.

As my mom drew, she tried to get me to spill my guts to her, you know, about what Lana said that made me go on a cell-phone-stomping rampage. You could tell she was trying really hard to be all TV mom about it.

I guess it must have worked, because all of a sudden I found myself telling her all of it, every last thing: the stuff about Kenny and about my not liking to kiss him and about him telling everybody, and about how I plan to break up with him as soon as finals are over.

And along the way, I mentioned Michael and Judith Gershner and Tina and the greeting cards and the Winter Carnival and Lilly and her protest group and how I'm secretary of it, and just about everything else, except the part about pulling the fire alarm.

After a while my mom stopped drawing and just looked at me.

Finally, when I was done, she said, "You know what I think you need?"

And I said, "What?"

And she said, "A vacation."

So then we had a sort of vacation, right there on her bed. I mean, she wouldn't let me go study. Instead, she made me order a pizza, and together we watched the satisfying but completely unbelievable end of *Mother, May I Sleep with Danger?*, which was followed, much to our joy, by the dishiest made-for-TV movie ever, *Midwest Obsession*, in which Courtney Thorne-Smith plays the local Dairy Princess, who goes around in a pink Cadillac wearing cow earrings and kills people like Tracey Gold (deep in the throes of her post–*Growing Pains* anorexia) for messing with her boyfriend. And the best part was, it was all *based on a true story*.

For a while, there on my mom's bed, it was almost

like old times. You know, before my mom met Mr. Gianini and I found out I was a princess.

Except, of course, not really, because she's pregnant, and I'm suspended.

But why quibble?

Friday, December 12, 8 p.m., the loft

Oh, my God, I just checked my e-mail. I am being inundated with supportive messages from my friends!

They all want to congratulate me on my decisive handling of Lana Weinberger. They sympathize with my suspension and encourage me to stay firm in my refusal to back down from my stand against the administration (what stand against the administration? All I did was destroy a cell phone. It has nothing to do with the administration). Lilly went so far as to compare me with Mary, Queen of Scots, who was imprisoned and then beheaded by Elizabeth I.

I wonder if Lilly would still think that if she knew that the reason I smashed Lana's cell phone was because she was threatening to spill the beans about my having pulled the fire alarm that ruined Lilly's walkout.

Lilly says it's all a matter of principle, that I was banished from the school for refusing to back down from my beliefs. But actually, I was banished from school for destroying someone else's private property— and I only did it to cover up for another crime that I committed.

No one knows that but me, though. Well, me and Lana. And even she doesn't know for sure why I did it. I mean, it could have been just one of those random acts of violence that are going around.

Everyone else, however, is seeing it as this great

political act. Tomorrow, at the first meeting of the Students Against the Corporatization of Albert Einstein High School, my case is going to be held up as an example of one of the many unjust decisions of the Gupta Administration.

I think tomorrow I might develop a case of weekend strep throat.

Anyway, I wrote back to everyone, telling them how much I appreciate their support, and not to make a bigger deal out of this than it actually is. I mean, I'm not proud of what I did. I would much rather have NOT done it, and stayed in school.

One bright note: Michael is definitely getting the cards I've been sending him. Tina walked by his locker today after PE and saw him take the latest one out and put it in his backpack! Unfortunately, according to Tina, he did not wear an expression of dazed passion as he slipped the card into his bag, nor did he gaze at it tenderly. He did not even put it away very carefully: Tina regretted to inform me that he slipped his iMac laptop into his backpack next, undoubtedly squashing the card.

But he wouldn't, Tina hastened to assure me, have done that if he'd known it was from you, Mia! Maybe if you'd signed it . . .

But if I signed it, he'd know I like him! More than that, he'd know I love him, since I do believe the L word was mentioned in at least one card. And what if he doesn't feel the same way about me? How embarrassing! Way worse than being suspended.

Oh, no! As I was writing this, I got Instant Messaged by, of all people, Michael himself! I freaked out so bad, I shrieked and scared Fat Louie, who was sleeping on my lap as I wrote. He sank all of his claws into me, and now I have little puncture marks all over my thighs.

Michael wrote:

CRACKING: Hey, Thermopolis, what's this I hear about you getting suspended?

I wrote back:

FTLOUIE: Just for one day.

CRACKING: What'd you do?

FTLOUIE: Crushed a cheerleader's cellular phone.

CRACKING: Your parents must be so proud.

FTLOUIE: If so, they've done a pretty good job of disguising it so far.

CRACKING: So are you grounded?

FTLOUIE: Surprisingly, no. The attack on the cell phone was provoked.

CRACKING: So you'll still be going to the Carnival next week?

FTLOUIE: As secretary to the Students Against the Corporatization of Albert Einstein High School, I believe my attendance is required. Your sister is planning for us to have a booth.

CracKing: That Lilly. She's always looking out for the good of mankind.

FtLouie: That's one way of putting it.

We probably would have talked longer, but right then my mom yelled at me to get off line, since she's waiting to hear from Mr. Gianini, who, surprisingly, still wasn't home from school, even though it was past dinnertime. So I logged off.

This is the second time Michael's asked if I'm going to the Winter Carnival. What's up with that?

Friday, December 12, 9 p.m., the loft

Now we know why Mr. G was so late getting home:
He stopped along the way to buy a Christmas tree.

Not just any Christmas tree, either, but a twelve-
footer that must be at least six feet wide at the base.

I didn't say anything negative, of course, because
my mom was so happy and excited about it, and immediately lugged out all of her Dead Celebrity Christmas
ornaments (my mom doesn't use pretty glass balls or
tinsel on her Christmas tree, like normal people.
Instead, she paints pieces of tin with the likenesses of
celebrities who have died that year, and hangs those on
the tree. Which is why we probably have the only tree
in North America with ornaments commemorating
Richard and Pat Nixon, Elvis, Audrey Hepburn, Kurt
Cobain, Jim Henson, John Belushi, Rock Hudson,
Alec Guiness, Divine, John Lennon, and many, many
more).

And Mr. Gianini kept looking over at me, to see if
I was happy, too. He got the tree, he said, because he
knew what a bad day I'd had, and he didn't want it to
be a total loss.

Mr. G, of course, has no idea what my English term
paper topic is.

What was I supposed to say? I mean, he'd already
gone out and bought it, and you know a tree that size
had to have cost a lot of money. And he'd meant to do

a nice thing. He really had.

Still, I wish the people around here would consult me about things before just going out and doing them. Like the whole pregnancy thing, and now this tree. If Mr. G had asked me, I would have been like, Let's go to the Big Kmart on Astor Place and get a nice fake tree so we don't contribute to the destruction of the polar bear's natural habitat, okay?

Only he didn't ask me.

And the truth is, even if he had, my mom would never have gone for it. Her favorite part of Christmas is lying on the floor with her head under the tree, gazing up through the branches and inhaling the sweet tangy smell of pine sap. She says it's the only memory of her Indiana childhood she actually likes.

It's hard to think about the polar bears when your mom says something like that.

Well, the first meeting of the Students Against the Corporatization of Albert Einstein High School is a complete bust.

That's because nobody showed up but me and Boris Pelkowski. I am a little miffed that Kenny didn't come. You would think that if he really loves me as much as he says he does, he would take any opportunity whatsoever to be near me, even a boring meeting of the Students Against the Corporatization of Albert Einstein High School.

But I guess even Kenny's love is not that great. As should be obvious to me by now, considering the fact that there are exactly six days until the Nondenominational Winter Dance, and Kenny STILL HASN'T ASKED ME IF I WANT TO GO WITH HIM.

Not that I'm worried, or anything. I mean, a girl who set off a fire alarm AND smashed Lana Weinberger's cell phone, worried about not having a date to a stupid dance?

All right. I'm worried.

But not worried enough to pull a Sadie Hawkins and ask *him* to the dance.

Lilly is pretty much inconsolable over the fact that no one but Boris and me showed up for her meeting. I tried to tell her that everybody is too busy studying for finals to worry about privatization at the moment, but she doesn't seem to care. Right now she is sitting on the couch, with Boris speaking to her in a soothing voice. Boris is pretty gross and all—with his sweaters that he always tucks into his pants, and that weird retainer his orthodontist makes him wear—but you can tell he genuinely loves Lilly. I mean, look at the tender way he is gazing at her as she sobs about how she is going to call her congressmember.

It makes my heart hurt, looking at Boris looking at Lilly.

I guess I must be jealous. I want a boy to look at *me* like that. And I don't mean Kenny, either. I mean a boy who I actually like back, as more than just a friend.

I can't take it anymore. I am going into the kitchen to see what Maya, the Moscovitzes' housekeeper, is doing. Even helping to wash things has to be better than this.

Maya wasn't in the kitchen. She was here, in Michael's room, putting away his school uniform, which she just finished ironing. Maya is going around picking up Michael's things and telling me about her son Manuel. Thanks to the help of the Drs. Moscovitz, Manuel was recently released from the prison in the Dominican Republic where he'd been wrongfully held for suspicion of having committed crimes against the state. Now Manuel is starting his own political party, and Maya is just as proud as can be, except she is worried he might end up back in prison if he doesn't tone down the anti-government stuff a little.

Manuel and Lilly have a lot in common, I guess.

Maya's stories about Manuel are always interesting, but it is much more interesting to be in Michael's room. I have been in it before, of course, but never while he was gone (he is at school, even though it is Saturday, working in the computer lab on his project for the Carnival; apparently the school's modem is faster than his. Also, I suppose, though I hate to admit it, he and Judith Gershner can freely practice their downloading there, without fear of parental interruption).

So I am lying on Michael's bed while Maya putters around, folding shirts and muttering about sugar, one of her native land's main exports and apparently a source of some consternation to her son's political platform, while Michael's dog, Pavlov, sits next to me, panting on my face. I can't help thinking, *This is what it's like to be Michael: This is what Michael sees when he looks up at his ceiling at night* (he has put glow-in-the-dark stars up there, in the form of the spiral galaxy Andromeda) and *This is how Michael's sheets smell* (springtime fresh, thanks to the detergent Maya uses) and *This is what the view of Michael's desk looks like from his bed.*

Except that looking over at his desk, I just noticed something. It's one of my cards! The one with the strawberry on it!

It isn't exactly on display, or anything. It's just sitting on his desk. But hey, that's a far cry from being crumpled at the bottom of his backpack. It shows that the cards mean something to him, that he hasn't buried them under all the other junk on his desk—the DOS manuals and anti-Microsoft literature—or worse, thrown them away.

This is somewhat heartening.

Uh-oh. I just heard the front door open. Michael??? Or the Drs. Moscovitz???? I better get out of here. Michael doesn't have all those Enter At Your Own Risk signs on the door for nothing.

Saturday, December 13, 3 p.m., Grandmère's

How, you might ask, did I go from the Moscovitzes' apartment to my grandmother's suite at the Plaza in the space of a mere half hour?

Well, I'll tell you.

Disaster has struck, in the form of Sebastiano.

I always suspected, of course, that Sebastiano was not the sweet-tempered innocent he pretended to be. But now it looks like the only murder Sebastiano needs to worry about is his own. Because if my dad ever gets his hands on him, Sebastiano is one dead fashion designer.

Looking at it objectively, I think I can safely say I'd prefer to have been murdered. I mean, I'd be dead and all, which would be sad—especially since I still haven't written down those instructions for caring for Fat Louie while I'm gone—but at least I wouldn't have to show up for school on Monday.

But now, not only do I have to show up for school on Monday, but I have to show up for school on Monday knowing that every single one of my fellow classmates is going to have seen the supplement that arrived in the *Sunday Times*: the supplement featuring about twenty photos of ME standing in front of a triple mirror in dresses by Sebastiano, with the words "Fashion Fit for a Princess" emblazoned all over the place.

Oh, yes. I'm not kidding. Fashion Fit for a Princess.

I can't really blame him, I guess. Sebastiano, I mean. I suppose the opportunity was too much for him to resist. He is, after all, a businessman, and having a princess model your clothes . . . well, you can't buy exposure like that.

Because you know all the other papers are going to pick up on the story. You know, Princess of Genovia Makes Modeling Debut. That kind of thing.

So with just one little photo spread, Sebastiano is going to get virtual worldwide coverage of his new clothing line.

A clothing line that it looks like I have endorsed.

Grandmère doesn't understand why my dad and I are so upset. Well, I think she gets why my dad is upset. You know the whole "My daughter is being used" thing. She just doesn't get why *I'm* so unhappy. "You look perfectly beautiful," she keeps saying.

Yeah. Like that helps.

Grandmère thinks I am overreacting. But hello, have I ever aspired to tread in Claudia Schiffer's footsteps? I don't think so. Fashion is so not what I'm about. What about the environment? What about the rights of animals? What about the HORSESHOE CRABS??????

People are not going to believe I didn't pose for those photos. People are going to think I am a sellout. People are going to think I am a stuck-up model snob.

I would so rather that they think I am a juvenile delinquent, I can't tell you.

Little did I know when I heard the front door to the Moscovitzes' apartment opening, and I hustled out of Michael's room, that I was about to be greeted by the disastrous news. It was only Lilly's parents, after all, coming home from the gym, where they'd met with their personal trainers. Afterward, they'd stopped to have a latte and read the *Sunday Times*, large sections of which arrive, for reasons no one understands, on Saturday, if you have a subscription.

What a surprise they had had, when they'd opened up the paper and saw the Princess of Genovia hawking this hot new fashion designer's spring collection.

What a surprise I had, when the Drs. Moscovitz congratulated me on my new modeling career, and I was all, "What are you talking about?"

So, while Lilly and Boris looked on with curiosity, Dr. Moscovitz opened her paper and showed me:

And there it was, in all of its four-color-layout glory.

I'm not going to lie and say I looked bad. I looked okay. What they had done was, they had taken all the photos Sebastiano's assistant had snapped of me trying to decide which dress to wear to my introduction to the people of Genovia and laid them all out on this purple background. I'm not smiling in the pictures, or anything. I'm just looking at myself in the mirror, clearly going, in my head, *Ew, could I look more like a walking toothpick?*

But of course, if you didn't know me, and didn't know WHY I was trying on all these dresses, I'd seem like some freak who cares WAY too much about how she looks in a party dress.

Which is exactly the kind of person I've always wanted to be portrayed as.

NOT!!!!!!!

I have to admit, I am a little hurt. I'd thought, when he'd asked me all those questions about Michael, Sebastiano and I had kind of made a connection. But I guess not. Not if he could do something like this.

My dad has already called the *Times* and demanded that they remove the supplement from all the papers that haven't been delivered yet. He has called the concierge of the Plaza and insisted on Sebastiano being listed as persona non grata, which means the cousin to the prince of Genovia won't be allowed to set foot on hotel property.

I thought this was a little harsh, but not as harsh as what my dad *wanted* to do, which was call the NYPD and press charges against Sebastiano for using the likeness of a minor without the consent of her parents. Thank God Grandmère talked him out of that. She said there'd be enough publicity about this without the added humiliation of a royal arrest.

My dad is still so mad he can't sit still. He is pacing back and forth across the suite. Rommel is watching him very nervously from Grandmère's lap, his head moving back and forth, back and forth, his eyes following my dad as if he were watching the US Open or something.

I bet if Sebastiano *were* here, my dad would smash up a lot more than just his cell phone.

Well.

All I can say is, Grandmère's really done it this time.

I'm serious. I don't think my dad is ever going to speak to her again.

And I know *I* never will.

And okay, she's an old lady and she didn't know that what she was doing was wrong, and I should really be more understanding.

But for her to do *this*—for her not to even take into consideration my feelings—I frankly don't think I will ever be able to forgive her.

What happened was, Sebastiano called right before I was getting ready to leave the hotel. He was completely perplexed about why my dad is so mad at him. He tried to come upstairs to see us, he said, but Plaza security stopped him.

When my dad, who'd answered the phone, told Sebastiano that the reason Plaza security stopped him was because he'd been PNG'd, and then explained why, Sebastiano was even more upset. He kept going, "But I had your permish! I had your permish, Phillipe!"

"My permission to use my daughter's image to promote your tawdry rags?" My father was disgusted. "You most certainly did not!"

But Sebastiano kept insisting he had.

And little by little, it came out that he *had* had permission, in a way. Only not from me. And not my dad, either. Guess who, it appears, gave it to him?

Grandmère went, all indignantly, "I only did it, Phillipe, because Amelia, as you know, suffers from a terrible self-image, and needed a boost."

But my dad was so enraged, he wouldn't even listen to her. He just thundered, "And so to repair her self-image, you went behind her back and gave permission for her photo to be used in an advertisement for *women's clothing?*"

Grandmère didn't have much to say after that. She just stood there, going "Uhn . . . uhn . . . uhn . . ." like someone in a horror movie who'd been pinned to a wall with a machete but wasn't quite dead yet (I always close my eyes during parts like this, so I know exactly what it sounds like).

It became clear that even if Grandmère had had a reasonable excuse for her behavior, my father wasn't going to listen to it—or let me listen to it, either. He stalked over to me, grabbed my arm, and marched me right out of the suite.

I thought we were going to have a bonding moment, like fathers and daughters always do on TV, where he'd tell me that Grandmère was a very sick woman and that he was going to send her somewhere where she could take a nice, long rest, but instead all he said was, "Go home."

Then he handed me over to Lars—after slamming the door to Grandmère's suite VERY loudly behind him, before storming off in the direction of his own suite.

Jeez.

It just goes to show, even a royal family can be dysfunctional.

Couldn't you just see us on *Ricki Lake*?

Ricki: Clarisse, tell us: Why did you allow
            Sebastiano to put your granddaughter's
            photos in that *Times* advertising
            supplement?
Grandmère: That's Your Royal Highness to you, Ms.
            Lake. I did it to boost her self-esteem.

I just know that when I get to school on Monday, everybody is going to be all, "Oh, look, here comes Mia, that big FAKE, with her vegetarianism and her animal-rights activism and her looks-aren't-important-it's-what's-on-the-inside-that-matters-ism. But I guess it's all right to pose for *fashion photo shoots*, isn't it, Mia?"

As if it wasn't enough to be suspended. Now I am going to be sneered at by my peers, too.

I'm home now, trying to pretend none of it ever happened. This is difficult, of course, because when I walked back into the loft, I saw that my mom had already pulled the supplement out of our paper and drawn little devil horns coming out of my head in every picture, then stuck the whole thing onto the refrigerator.

While I appreciate this bit of whimsy, it does not make the fact that I will have to show my face—now plastered all over advertising supplements throughout the tristate area—in school on Monday any easier.

Surprisingly, there is one good thing that's come out of all of this: I know for sure I look best in the white taffeta number with the blue sash. My dad says over his dead body am I going to wear it, or any other Sebastiano creation, again. But there isn't another designer in Genovia who could do as good a job, let alone finish the dress in time. So it looks like the dress by Sebastiano, which got delivered to the loft this morning, is it.

Which is one thing off my mind, anyway.

I guess.

I've already gotten seventeen e-mails, six phone calls, and one visitor (Lilly) about the fashion thing. Lilly says it's not as bad as I think, and that most people throw the supplements away without even looking at them.

If that's true, I said, why are all these people calling and e-mailing me?

She tried to make out like it was all members of the Students Against the Corporatization of Albert Einstein High School, calling to show their solidarity with my suspension, but I think we both know better:

It's all people who want to know what I was thinking, selling out like that.

How am I ever going to explain that I had nothing to do with it, that I didn't even *know* about it? Nobody is going to believe that. I mean, the proof is right there: I'm *wearing* the proof. There's photographic evidence of it.

My reputation is going down the drain, even as I sit here. Tomorrow morning, millions of subscribers to *The New York Times* are going to open their papers and be like, "Oh, look, Princess Mia. Sold out already. Wonder how much she got paid? You wouldn't think she'd need the money, what with being royal, and all."

Finally I had to ask Lilly to please go home, because I'd developed a bad headache. She tried to cure it with some shiatsu, which her parents frequently employ on their patients, but it didn't work. All that ended up happening was that I think she burst a blood vessel or something between my thumb and index finger, since it really hurts.

Now I am determined to start studying, even though it's Saturday night, and everyone else my age is out having fun.

But haven't you heard? Princesses never get to have any fun.

HERE IS WHAT I HAVE TO DO

Algebra: review Chapters 1–10
English: term paper, 10 pages, double spaced; utilize appropriate margins; also, review Chapters 1–7
World Civ: review Chapters 1–12
G & T: none
French: revue Chapitres Un–Neuf
Biology: review Chapters 1–12
Write out instructions on how to care for Fat Louie
Christmas/Hannukah shopping:

       Mom—Bon Jovi maternity T
       Dad—Book on anger management
       Mr. G—Swiss Army knife
       Lilly—blank videotapes
       Tina Hakim Baba—copy of *Emanuelle*
       Kenny—combination TV/VCR (I don't think

this is too extravagant. And no, it's not
guilt, either. He really wants one.)
Grandmère—NOTHING!!!!!!

Paint fingernails (maybe presence of foul-tasting
polish will prevent biting them off)
Break up with Kenny
Organize sock drawer

I am going to start with the sock drawer, because
that is clearly the most important. You can't really concentrate on anything if your socks aren't right.

Then I will move on to Algebra because that is my
worst subject, and also my first test. I am going to pass
it if it's the last thing I do. NOTHING is going to distract me. Not this thing with Grandmère, not the fact
that four of those seventeen e-mails are from Michael,
not the fact that two are from Kenny, not the fact that
I am leaving for Europe at the end of next week, not
the fact that my mother and Mr. Gianini are in the next
room watching *Die Hard*, my favorite Christmas movie,
NOTHING.

I WILL PASS ALGEBRA THIS SEMESTER,
and NOTHING IS GOING TO DISTRACT ME
FROM STUDYING FOR THE FINAL!!!!!!!!!!!!

Saturday, December 13, 9 p.m., the loft

I just had to go out and see the part where Bruce Willis throws the explosives down the elevator shaft, but now I am back at work.

Saturday, December 13, 9:30 p.m., the loft

I was really curious about what Michael could possibly want, so I read his e-mails—just his. One was about the supplement (Lilly had told him, and he wanted to know if I was thinking of abdicating, ha ha) and the other three were jokes that I guess were supposed to make me feel better. They weren't very funny, but I laughed anyway.

I bet Judith Gershner doesn't laugh at Michael's jokes. She's too busy cloning things.

HOW TO CARE FOR FAT LOUIE
WHILE I AM AWAY

A.M.:

In the morning, please fill Fat Louie's bowl with DRY FOOD. Even if there is already food in the bowl, he likes to have some fresh served on top so he can feel like he is having breakfast like the rest of us.

In my bathroom is a BLUE PLASTIC CUP sitting by the bathtub. Please fill that every morning with water from the bathroom sink. You must use water from the bathroom sink, because water from the kitchen sink isn't cold enough. And you have to put it in the BLUE CUP because that is the cup Fat Louie is used to drinking out of while I am brushing my teeth.

He has a bowl in the hallway outside my room. Rinse that out and fill it with water from the WATER FILTER PITCHER in the refrigerator. It must be water from the WATER FILTER PITCHER because even though New York tap is said to be contaminant-free, it is good for Louie to get at least some water that is definitely pure. Cats need to drink a lot of water to flush out their systems and prevent kidney and urinary tract infections, so always leave lots of water out, and not just by his food bowls, but other places as well.

Do not confuse the bowl in the hall with the BOWL BY THE CHRISTMAS TREE. That bowl is there to discourage Louie from drinking out of the tree holder. Too much tree resin could make him constipated.

In the morning, Fat Louie likes to sit on the windowsill in my room and look at the pigeons on the fire escape. NEVER OPEN THIS WINDOW, but be sure the curtains are open so he can see out.

Also, sometimes he likes to look out the windows by the TV. If he cries while he is doing this, it means you should pet him.

P.M.:

At dinnertime, give Fat Louie CANNED FOOD. Fat Louie only likes three flavors: CHICKEN AND TUNA FEAST (FLAKED), SHRIMP AND FISH FEAST (FLAKED), and OCEAN FISH FEAST (FLAKED). He won't eat anything with BEEF or PORK. He must have the contents of the can on a new, CLEAN saucer, or he won't eat. Also, he won't eat if the contents don't retain their CANLIKE SHAPE on the plate, so don't chop up his food.

After eating his canned food, Fat Louie likes to stretch out on the carpet in front of the front door. This is a good time to give him his exercise. When he stretches out, just put your hand under his front legs and straighten them (he likes this) until he bends like a comma. Then dig your thumbs between his shoulder blades and give him a kitty massage. He will purr if you do it right. If you do it wrong you will know, because he will bite you.

Fat Louie gets bored very easily, and when he gets bored, he walks around crying, so here are some games he likes to play:

Take some pieces of CAT TREAT and line them up on top of the stereo for Fat Louie to knock off and chase.

Put Fat Louie in my COMPUTER CHAIR and then hide behind the bookshelf and throw one end of a shoelace over the back of the chair so he can't see where it is coming from.

Make a FORT out of pillows on my bed and put Fat Louie inside of it and then stick your hand into any openings between the pillows (I recommend wearing an oven mitt during this game).

Put some catnip in an OLD SOCK and throw
it to Fat Louie. Then leave him alone for four
to five hours, because catnip makes him a
little free with his claws.

THE LITTER BOX

Mr. Gianini, this one is for you. Mom must not
clean out the litter box or touch anything that may have
come in contact with it, or she might develop toxoplas-
mosis, and the baby might get sick. Always wash your
hands in warm, soapy water after changing Fat Louie's
litter box, even if you don't think you got anything on
your hands.

Fat Louie's box needs to be scooped out EVERY
DAY. Always use clumping litter, and then just scoop
out the clumps into a Grand Union bag and dispose.
Nothing could be simpler. He tends to do number 2
about two hours after his evening meal. You will be able
to tell from the odor wafting from his box in my bathroom.

MOST IMPORTANT OF ALL

Remember not to disturb Fat Louie's SPECIAL
AREA BEHIND THE TOILET in my bathroom.
That is where he keeps his collection of shiny objects.

If he takes something of yours and you find it there, be sure not to take it out while he is looking, or for weeks he will try to bite you every time he sees you. I talked to the vet about it, but she said short of hiring an animal behaviorist at $70/hr there is nothing that can be done. We just have to put up with it.

ABOVE ALL, BE SURE TO PICK FAT LOUIE UP SEVERAL TIMES A DAY AND HUG AND SQUEEZE HIM!!!!! (HE LIKES THIS.)

Saturday, December 13, Midnight, the loft

I can't believe it's midnight already, and I am still only on Chapter One of *An Introduction to Algebra*!

This book is incomprehensible. I sincerely hope whoever wrote it did not make very much money off of it.

I should just go and ask Mr. G what's going to be on the final.

No, that would be cheating.

Wouldn't it?

Sunday, December 14, 10 a.m., the loft

Only forty-eight hours until the Algebra final, and I am still on Chapter One.

Lilly just came over again. She wants to study for World Civ together. I told her I can't worry about World Civ when I am only on Chapter One in my Algebra review, but she said we could alternate: She would quiz me on Algebra for an hour, then I could quiz her on World Civ for an hour. I said okay, even though it really isn't fair: She is getting an A in Algebra, so her quizzing me isn't really helping her any, while my quizzing her in World Civ helps me study for it, too.

But that's what friends are for, I guess.

Sunday, December 14, 11 a.m., the loft

Tina just called. Her little brother and sisters are driving her crazy. She wanted to know if she could come down and study here. I said sure.

What else could I say? Besides, she promised to stop at H and H for bagels and vegetable cream cheese. And she said she thought the photos of me in the supplement were beautiful and that I shouldn't care if people call me a sellout, because I look so hot.

Sunday, December 14, Noon, the loft

Michael told Boris where Lilly is, so now Boris is here, too.

Lilly's right. Boris really does breathe too loudly. It's very distracting.

And I wish he wouldn't put his feet on my bed. The least he could do is take his shoes off first. But when I suggested it, Lilly said that would be a bad idea.

Ew. I don't know why Lilly puts up with a boyfriend who is not only a mouth breather but also has stinky feet.

Boris may be a musical genius, but he has a lot to learn about hygiene, if you ask me.

Sunday, December 14, 12:30 p.m., the loft

Now Kenny's here. I don't know how I am supposed to get any studying done with all of these people
around. Plus, Mr. Gianini has decided that now would
be a good time to practice his drums.

I told Lilly, and she agreed, that once Boris and Kenny showed up, the whole studying thing kind of went down the drain. Plus, Mr. G's drumming didn't help. So we decided it would be best to take a study break and go to Chinatown for dim sum.

We had a good time at Great Shanghai eating vegetable dumplings and dried sauteed string beans with garlic sauce. I ended up sitting by Boris, and he really made me laugh, engineering it so that whenever the waiters brought something new, the only empty spot on the table was in front of him, so they had to put it there, and then Boris and I got first dibs on it.

Which made me realize that in spite of the sweaters and the mouth-breathing, Boris really is a funny and nice person. Lilly is so lucky. I mean, that the boy she loves actually loves her back. If only I could love Kenny the way Lilly loves Boris!

But I don't seem to have any control over who I fall in love with. Believe me, if I did, I would NOT love Michael. I mean, for one thing, he is my best friend's older brother, and if Lilly ever found out I liked him, she would NOT understand. Also, of course, he is a senior and is graduating soon.

And oh, yeah, he already has a girlfriend.

But what am I supposed to do? I can't *make* myself fall in love with Kenny any more than I can *make* him stop liking me, you know, in that special way.

Although he still hasn't asked me to the dance. Or mentioned it, anyway. Lilly says I should just call him and be like, "So are we going, or not?" After all, she keeps pointing out, I had the guts to smash up Lana's cell phone. Why don't I have the guts to call my own boyfriend and ask him whether or not he is taking me to the school dance?

But I smashed up Lana's cell phone in the heat of passion. I cannot summon up anything like passion where Kenny is concerned. There is a part of me that doesn't want to go to the dance with him at all, and that part of me is relieved that he hasn't mentioned anything about it.

Okay, it is a very small part of me, but it's still *there*.

So actually, even though I was having fun sitting by Boris at the restaurant and all, it was also a little depressing, on account of the whole Kenny thing.

And then things got even more depressing. That's because some little Chinese-American girls came up to me as I was opening my fortune cookie and wanted to know if they could have my autograph. Then they handed me pens and the advertising supplement that had appeared in that day's *Times* for me to sign.

I seriously thought about killing myself, only I couldn't think how I'd do it, except for maybe stabbing myself through the heart with a chopstick.

Instead I just signed the stupid thing for them and

tried to smile. But inside, of course, I was FREAKING OUT, especially when I saw how happy the little girls were to have met me. And why? No, not because of my tireless work on behalf of the polar bears or the whales or starving kids. Which I haven't actually done yet, but I fully intend to do.

No, because I'd been in a magazine in a bunch of pretty dresses, and I'm tall and skinny like a model.

Which is no accomplishment at all!

After that, my headache came back, and I said I had to go home.

Nobody protested very much, I think because everybody realized all of a sudden how much time we'd wasted, and how much studying we all had left to do. So we left, and now I am home again, and my mom says that while I was gone, Sebastiano called four times, AND he had another dress delivered.

Not just any dress, either. It is a dress Sebastiano designed just for me, to wear to the Nondenominational Winter Dance. It's not sexy. It isn't sexy at all. It's dark green velvet with long sleeves and a wide, square neckline.

But when I put it on and looked at my reflection in the mirror in my room, something funny happened:

I looked good. *Really* good.

There was a note attached to the dress that said,

Please forgive me.
I promise this dress will not make him think of you
as his little sister's best friend.

    S.

Which is very sweet. Sad, but sweet. Sebastiano can't know, of course, that the Michael situation is completely hopeless, and that no *dress* is going to make any difference, no matter how nice I look in it.

But hey, at least Sebastiano *apologized*. That's a lot more, I've noticed, than Grandmère has done.

Of course I forgive Sebastiano. I mean, none of it is his fault, really.

And I guess someday I'll probably forgive Grandmère, since she's too old to know any better.

But the person I will never, ever forgive is myself, for getting into this situation in the first place. I totally should have known better. I should have told Sebastiano, No photos, please. Only I was so carried away, looking at myself in all those beautiful dresses, that I forgot that being a princess is more than just wearing pretty dresses: It's being an example to a lot of people . . . people you don't even know and may not ever even meet.

Which is why if I don't pass this Algebra test, I am dead.

Here are the number of students at Albert Einstein High School who (so far) have felt compelled to make comments to me about my smashing Lana Weinberger's cell phone last Friday: 37

Here are the number of students at Albert Einstein High School who (so far) have felt compelled to mention my suspension last Friday: 59

Here are the number of students at Albert Einstein High School who (so far) have felt compelled to make comments to me about my appearance in an advertising supplement to *The New York Times* over the weekend: 74

Total number of comments made to me so far today by students at Albert Einstein High School: 170

Oddly, after wading through all of this, when I got to my locker, I found something that seemed extremely out of place: a single yellow rose, sticking out of the door.

What can this mean? Can there be someone in this school who does not despise me?

Apparently so. But when I looked around, wondering who my one supporter could be, I saw only Justin Baxendale, being stalked (as usual) by a horde of worshipful girls.

I suppose my anonymous rose-leaver must be Kenny, trying to cheer me up. He will not admit it, but who else could it be?

It is Reading Day today, which means we are supposed to spend the whole day—except for lunch—sitting in Homeroom, studying for our finals, which begin tomorrow. This is fine by me, since at least this way, there's no chance I'll run into Lana. Her homeroom is on a whole other floor.

The only problem is that Kenny's in this class. We have to sit alphabetically, so he's way up at the front of this row, but he keeps passing notes back to me. Notes that say things like, *Keep on smilin'!* and *Hang in there, Sunshine!*

He won't fess up to the rose thing, though.

By the way, want to know the total number of comments made to me so far today by Michael Moscovitz? 1

And it wasn't even really a comment. He told me in the hallway that my combat boot had come untied.

And it had.

My life is so over.

Four days until the Nondenominational Winter Dance, and still no date.

Distance formula: $d - 10xrt$

$r = 10$
$t = 2$
$d = 10 + (10)(2)$
$\ \ = 10 + 20 = 30$

Variables are placeholders for numbers (letters)
Distributive law
$5x + 5y - 5$
$5 (x + y - 1)$

$2a - 2b + 2c$
$2 (-1) - 2(-2) + 2 (5)$
$-2 + 4 + 10 = 12$

Four times a number is added to three. The result is five times the number.

Find the number.

$x = $ the number
$\ \ 4x + 3\ \ = 5x$
$\underline{-4x \qquad\quad -4x}$
$\qquad\quad 3 = x$

Regardes les oisseaux stupides.

Cartesian coordinate system divides the plane into four parts called quadrants

Quadrant 1 (positive, positive)
Quadrant 2 (negative, positive)
Quadrant 3 (negative, negative)
Quadrant 4 (positive, negative)

Slope: slope of a line is line denoted m

Find slope
negative slopes
positive slopes
zero slope
Vertical line has no slope
Horizontal line has 0 slope
Collinear—points that lie on the same line
Parallel lines have the same slope

$$4x + 2y = 6$$
$$2y = -4x + 6$$
$$y = -2x + 3$$

Active voice indicates that the subject of the verb is acting

Passive voice indicates that the subject of the verb is being acted upon

Tuesday, December 16

Algebra and English finals completed.
Only three more, plus term paper, to go.

76 comments today, 53 of them negative:
"Sellout" = 29 times
I-Must-Think-I'm-All-That = 14 times
Here Comes Miss Thang = 6 times

Lilly says, "Who cares what people are saying? You
know the truth, right? And that's all that matters."

That's easy for Lilly to say. Lilly's not the one who
people are saying all those mean things about. *I* am.

Somebody left another yellow rose in my locker.
What is up with that? I asked Kenny again if it was him,
but he denied it. Strangely, he seemed to get very red
in the face about it. But this might have been because
Justin Baxendale, who was walking by at the time,
stepped on Kenny's foot. Kenny has very large feet,
larger even than mine.

Three more days until the Nondenominational
Winter Dance, and nada on the date front.

Wednesday, December 17

World Civ exam *finis*.
Two more, plus term paper, to go.

62 comments, 34 negative:
Don't give up your day job = 12 times
Sellout = 5 times
"If I was flat-chested like you, Mia, I could be a model, too" = 6 times

One rose, yellow, still no indication who left it. Perhaps someone is mistaking my locker for Lana's. She is, after all, always hanging out in that area, waiting for Josh Richter, whose locker is next door to mine, so that the two of them can suck face. It's possible that someone thinks he is leaving roses for her.

God knows no one at Albert Einstein High School would want to leave flowers for me. Unless I were dead, maybe, and they could fling them onto my grave and say, "Good riddance, Miss Thang."

Two more days until the dance. Still nothing.

Thursday, December 18, 1 a.m.

It just occurred to me:

Maybe Kenny is lying about the roses. Maybe they really *are* from him. Maybe he's leaving them as kind of teasers, leading up to asking me to the dance tomorrow night.

Which is kind of insulting, really. I mean, him waiting this long to finally ask. For all he knows, I could have said yes to somebody else by now.

As if somebody else might have asked.
HA!

THAT'S IT!!!!!
I'M DONE!!!!!!
DONE WITH FINALS!!!!!!!!!!!!!
And guess what?

I'm pretty sure I passed all of them. Even Algebra. The grades aren't posted until tomorrow, during the Winter Carnival, but I bugged Mr. G so much he finally said, "Mia, you did fine. Now leave me alone, all right?"

Got that????? He said I did FINE!!!!!!!!!! You know what *fine* means, don't you?

IT MEANS I PASSED!!!!!!!!!!!!!!!!

Thank God all of that's over. Now I can concentrate on what's important:

My social life.

I am serious. It is in a state of total disrepair. Everyone at school—with the exception of my friends—thinks I am this total sellout. They're like, "You talk the talk, Mia, but you don't walk the walk."

Well, I'm going to show them. Right after the World Civ exam yesterday, it hit me like a ton of bricks. I knew *exactly* what to do. It's what Grandmère would do.

Well, okay, maybe not *quite* what Grandmère would

do, but it will solve the whole problem. Granted, Sebastiano isn't going to like it very much. But then, he should have asked ME, not Grandmère, if it was all right to run those photos in an ad for his clothes. Right?

I have to say, this is the most princessy thing I've done so far. I am very, very nervous. Seriously. You wouldn't believe how much my palms are sweating.

But I cannot continue to lie back and meekly take this abuse. Something must be done about it, and I think I know what.

The best part is, I am doing it all by myself, with no help from anyone.

Well, all right, the concierge at the Plaza helped by getting me a room, and Lars helped by making all the calls on his cell phone.

And Lilly helped me write down what I was going to say, and Tina did my makeup and hair just now.

But other than that, it was all me.

Okay, we're here.

Here goes nothing.

I have now watched myself on all four major networks, plus New York 1, CNN, Headline News, MSNBC, and Fox News Channel. Apparently, they are also going to show it on *Entertainment Tonight*, *Access Hollywood*, and *E! Entertainment News*.

And I have to say, for a girl who supposedly has issues with her self-image, I think I did a fine job. I didn't mess up, not even once. If I maybe spoke a little too fast, well, you could still *understand* me. Unless, you know, you're a non–English-speaker or something.

I looked good, too. I probably should have worn something other than my school uniform, but you know, royal blue comes off pretty good on TV.

The phone has been ringing off the hook ever since the press conference was first aired. The first time it rang, my mom picked it up, and it was Sebastiano, screaming incomprehensibly about how I've ruined him.

Only he can't say ruined. It just came out "rued."

I felt really bad. I mean, I didn't mean to ruin him. Especially after he was so nice about designing me that dress for the dance.

But what was I supposed to do? I tried to make him look on the bright side:

"Sebastiano," I said, when I got on the phone, "I haven't ruined you. Really. It's just the proceeds from the sales of the dresses I'm wearing in the ad that will go to Greenpeace."

But Sebastiano completely failed to look at the big picture. He kept screaming, "Rued! I'm rued!"

I pointed out that, far from ruining him, his donating all the proceeds from sales of the dresses I modeled to Greenpeace was going to be perceived in the industry as a brilliant stroke of marketing genius, and that I wouldn't be surprised if those dresses flew off the racks, since girls like me, who are really the people his fashions are geared for, care a great deal about the environment.

I must have picked up a thing or two during my princess lessons with Grandmère, since in the end, I totally won him over. By the time I hung up, I think Sebastiano almost believed the whole thing had been his idea in the first place.

The next time the phone rang, it was my dad. I may have to scratch the plan to get him a book on anger management, because he was laughing his head off. He wanted to know if it had been my mom's idea, and when I said, "No, it was all me," he went, "You really *have* got the princess thing down, you know."

So, in a weird way, I feel like I passed that final, too.

Except of course that I'm still not speaking to Grandmère. Not a single one of the calls I've gotten tonight—from Lilly and Tina and Mamaw and Papaw back in Indiana, who saw the broadcast on a local affiliate—have been from her.

Really, I think she should be the one to apologize, because what she did was totally underhanded.

Almost as underhanded, my mom pointed out to me over dinner from Number One Noodle Son, as what *I* did.

Which is sort of shocking. I mean, I never thought about it before, but it's true: What I did tonight—it was as sneaky as anything Grandmère's ever done.

But I guess that shouldn't be very surprising. We *are* related, after all.

Then again, so were Luke Skywalker and Darth Vader.

Must go. *Baywatch* is on. This is the first time in a while I've been home to watch it.

Tina just called. She didn't want to talk about the press conference. She wanted to know what I got from my Secret Snowflake. I was all, "Secret Snowflake? What are you talking about?"

"You know," Tina said. "Your Secret Snowflake. You remember, Mia. We signed up for it like a month ago. You put your name in the jar, and then someone draws it, and they have to be your Secret Snowflake for the last week of school before Winter Break. They're supposed to surprise you with little gifts and stuff. You know, as a stress breaker. Since it's finals week, and all."

I dimly remembered, one day before Thanksgiving Break, Tina dragging me over to a folding table where some nerdy-looking kids from the student government were sitting on one side of the cafeteria with a big jar filled with little pieces of paper. Tina had made me write my name on a slip of paper, then pick someone else's name out of the jar.

"Oh, my God!" I cried. With all the stress of finals and everything, I had forgotten all about it!

Worse, I had forgotten that I had drawn Tina's name. No real coincidence, since she'd stuffed her slip of paper into the jar right before I picked. Still, what kind of heinous friend am I, that I would forget something like this?

Then I realized something else. The yellow roses. They hadn't been put in my locker by mistake! And they really weren't from Kenny, either! They had to be from my Secret Snowflake.

Which was kind of upsetting in a way. I mean, it's really starting to look as if Kenny has no intention whatsoever of asking me to tomorrow night's dance.

"I can't believe you forgot about it," Tina said, sounding amused. "You *have* been getting stuff for your Secret Snowflake, haven't you, Mia?"

I felt a rush of guilt. I had totally blown it. Poor Tina!

"Uh, sure," I said, wondering where I was going to find a present for her by tomorrow morning, the last day of the Secret Snowflake thing. "Sure, I have."

Tina sighed. "I guess nobody picked me," she said. "Because I haven't gotten anything."

"Oh, don't worry," I said, hoping the guilt washing over me wasn't noticeable in my voice. "You will. Your Secret Snowflake is probably waiting, you know, until the last day because she's—or he's—gotten you something really good."

"Do you think so?" Tina asked, wistfully.

"Oh, yes," I gushed.

Reassured, Tina got businesslike.

"Now," she said, "that finals are over . . ."

"Um, yes?"

". . . when are you going to tell Michael that you're

211

the one who sent him those cards?"

Shocked, I went, "How about never?"

To which Tina replied, tartly, "Mia, if you don't tell him, then what was the point of sending those cards?"

"To let him know that there are other girls out there who might like him, besides Judith Gershner."

Tina said, severely, "Mia, that's not enough. You've got to tell him it was you. How are you ever going to get him if he doesn't know how you feel?" Tina Hakim Baba, surprisingly, has a lot in common with my dad. "Remember Kenny? That's how Kenny got you. He sent the anonymous notes, but then he finally fessed up."

"Yeah," I said, sarcastically. "And look how great *that* turned out."

"It'll be different with you and Michael," Tina insisted. "Because you two are destined for each other. I can just *feel* it. You've got to tell him, and it's got to be tomorrow, because the next day, you are leaving for Genovia."

Oh, God. In my self-congratulations over having successfully maneuvered my first press conference, I'd forgotten about that, too. I am leaving for Genovia the day after tomorrow! With Grandmère! To whom I am not even speaking anymore!

I told Tina that I'd confess to Michael tomorrow. She hung up all happy.

But it was a good thing she hadn't been able to see my nostrils, because they were flaring like crazy, on account of the fact that I was totally lying to her.

Because there is no way I am ever telling Michael Moscovitz how I feel about him. No matter what my dad says. I *can't*.

Not to his face.

Not ever.

They are holding us hostage here in Homeroom until they've passed out our final semester grades. Then we are free to spend the rest of the day at the Winter Carnival in the gym, and then, later this evening, the dance.

Really. We don't have any more classes after this. We are just supposed to have fun.

As if. I am so never having fun again.

That is because—you know, aside from my many other problems, including the fact that I don't love my boyfriend, who also apparently does not love me any-more, at least not enough to ask me to the school dance, but I do love my best friend's brother, who is not even remotely aware of my feelings—that I think I know who my Secret Snowflake is.

Really, there is no other explanation. Why else would Justin Baxendale—who, even though he's so new, is still totally popular, not to mention way good-looking—be hanging around my locker so much? I mean, seriously. This is the third time I've spotted him lurking around there this week. Why else would he be hanging around there, except to leave those roses?

Unless he's planning on blackmailing me about the whole fire-alarm thing.

But Justin Baxendale doesn't exactly strike me as the blackmailer type. I mean, he looks to me like somebody who'd have something better to do than blackmail a princess.

Which leaves only one other explanation for why he could possibly be spending so much time around my locker: He is my Secret Snowflake.

And how totally embarrassing is it going to be when I go out there when the bell rings, and Justin comes up to me to confess—because that's the rule, it turns out: You have to reveal your identity to your Secret Snowflake today—and I have to look up into his smoky eyes with those long lashes and give a big fake smile and go, "Oh, gee, thanks, Justin. I had no idea it was you!"

Whatever. This is actually the least of my problems, right? I mean, considering that I am the only girl in this entire school who does not have a date to the dance tonight. And that tomorrow I have to leave for a country I am princess of, with my lunatic grandmother who isn't speaking to my father, and who, I know from past experience, is not above smoking in the airplane lavatory if the urge strikes her.

Really. Grandmère is a flight attendant's worst nightmare.

But that's not even half of it. I mean, what about my mom and Mr. Gianini? Sure, they're acting like they don't mind my spending the holidays in another country, and yes, we're going to have our own private little Christmas among ourselves before I leave, but really, I bet they mind. I bet they mind a lot.

And what about my grade in Algebra? Oh, Mr. Gianini says it's fine, but what is fine, exactly? A D? A D is not fine. Not considering the number of hours I've put into raising my grade from an F, it isn't. A D is *not* acceptable.

And what—oh God, *what*—am I going to do about Kenny?

At least I got Tina's present out of the way. I went on line last night and signed her up for a teen romance book-of-the-month club. I printed out the certificate, saying she is an official member, and will give it to her when the bell rings.

When the bell rings, which is also when I have to go out there and face Justin Baxendale.

It wouldn't be so bad if it weren't for those eyes of his. Why does he have to be so good-looking? And why did a good-looking person have to pick me as his Secret Snowflake? Beautiful people, like Lana and Justin, can't help but be repulsed by ordinary-looking people, like me.

He probably didn't even pull my name from that jar at all. Probably, he picked Lana's name and has been putting those roses in my locker, thinking it's Lana's, seeing as how God knows she never hangs out in front of her own locker.

What's even worse is, Tina told me yellow roses mean love *everlasting*.

Which of course was why I figured maybe it was Kenny after all.

Oh, great. They are passing around the printouts with our grades on them. I am not looking. I don't even care. I DO NOT CARE ABOUT MY GRADES.

Thank God for the bell. I'm just going to slip out of here—not looking at my grades, totally not looking at my grades—and go about my business like nothing out of the ordinary is going on.

Except of course when I get to my locker, Justin is there, looking for someone. Lana is there, too, waiting for Josh.

You know, I really don't need this. Justin revealing that he is my Secret Snowflake right in front of Lana, I mean. God only knows what she's going to say, the girl who has been suggesting I wear Band-Aids instead of a bra every day since the two of us hit puberty. Plus, it isn't like she's been super happy with me since the whole cell-phone thing. I'll bet she'll have something extra mean all prepared for the occasion. . . .

"Dude," Justin says.

Dude? I'm not a dude. Who is Justin talking to?

I turn around. Josh is standing there, behind Lana.

"Dude, I've been looking for you all week," Justin says, to Josh. "Do you have those Trig notes for me, or not? I've got to make up the final in one hour."

Josh says something, but I don't hear him. I don't

hear him because there's a roaring sound in my ears. There's a roaring sound in my ears because standing behind Justin is Michael. *Michael Moscovitz.*

And in his hand is *a yellow rose.*

Oh, God.

I am in so much trouble.

Again.

And it isn't even my fault this time. I mean, I couldn't help myself. It just *happened*, you know? And it doesn't mean anything. It was just, you know, one of those things.

And besides, it's not what Kenny thinks. Not even. I mean, if you think about it, it is a complete and total letdown. For me, anyway.

Because of course the first thing Michael says, when he sees me standing there gaping at him while he is holding that flower, is, "Here. This just fell out of your locker."

I took it from him in a complete daze. I swear to God my heart was beating so hard, I thought I was going to pass out.

Because I thought they'd been from him. The roses, I mean. For a minute there, I really did think Michael Moscovitz had been leaving me roses.

But of course this time, there's a note attached to the rose. It says:

Good luck on your trip to Genovia! See you when you get back!

Your Secret Snowflake,
Boris Pelkowski

Boris Pelkowski. Boris Pelkowski is the one who's been leaving those roses. Boris Pelkowski is my Secret Snowflake.

Of course Boris wouldn't know that a yellow rose represents love everlasting. Boris doesn't even know not to tuck his sweater into his pants. How would he know the secret language of flowers?

I don't know which was actually stronger, my feeling of relief that it wasn't Justin Baxendale leaving those roses after all . . .

. . . or my feeling of disappointment that it wasn't Michael.

Then Michael went, "Well? What's the verdict?"

To which I responded by staring at him blankly. I still hadn't quite gotten over it. You know, those brief few seconds when I'd thought—I'd actually thought, fool that I am—that he loved me.

"What did you get in Algebra?" he asked, slowly, as if I were dense.

Which, of course, I am. So dense that I never realized how much in love with Michael Moscovitz I was until Judith Gershner came along and swept him right out from under my nose.

Anyway, so I opened the computer printout containing my grades, and would you believe that I had raised my F in Algebra all the way up to a B minus?

Which just goes to show that if you spend nearly every waking moment in your life studying something, the likelihood is that you are going to retain at least a little of it.

Enough to get a B minus on the final, anyway.

I'm trying really hard not to gloat, but it's difficult. I mean, I'm so happy.

Well, except for the whole not-having-a-date-to-the-dance thing.

Still, it's hard to be unhappy. There is absolutely no way I got this grade because the teacher happens to be my stepfather. In Algebra, either you get the right answer, or you don't. There's nothing subjective about it, like in English. There's no interpretation of the facts. Either you're right, or you're not.

And I was right. Eighty percent of the time.

Of course it helped that I knew the answer to the final's extra-credit question: What instrument did Ringo, in the Beatles, play?

But that was only worth two points.

Anyway, here's the part where I got into trouble. Even though, of course, it isn't my fault.

I was so happy about my B minus, I completely forgot for a minute how much I am in love with Michael. I even forgot, for a change, to be shy around him. Instead, I did something really unlike me.

I threw my arms around him.

Seriously. Threw my arms right around his neck and went, "Wheeeeeeee!!!!!"

I couldn't help it. I was so happy. Okay, the whole

rose thing had been a little bit of a bummer, but the B minus made up for it. Well, almost.

It was just an innocent hug. That's *all* it was. Michael had, after all, tutored me almost the whole semester. He had some stake in that B minus, too.

But I guess Kenny, who Tina now tells me came around the corner right as I was doing it—hugging Michael, I mean—doesn't see it that way. According to Tina, Kenny thinks there's something going on between Michael and me.

To which, of course, I can only say, I WISH!

But I can't say that. I have to go find Kenny now, and let him know, you know, it was just a friendly hug.

Tina's all, "Why? Why don't you tell him the truth—that you don't feel the same way about him that he feels about you? This is your big chance!"

But you can't break up with someone during the Winter Carnival. I mean, really. How mean.

Why must my life be so fraught with trauma?

Well, I still haven't found Kenny, but I really have to hand it to the administrators: Grasping they might be, but they sure do know how to throw a party. Even Lilly is impressed.

Of course, signs of corporatization are everywhere: There are McDonald's orange drink dispensers on every floor, and it looks as if there was a run on Entenmann's, there are so many cake-and-cookie-laden tables scattered around.

Still, you can tell they are really trying to show us a good time. All of the clubs are offering activities and booths. There's ballroom dancing in the gym, courtesy of the Dance Club; fencing lessons in the auditorium, thanks to the Drama club; even cheerleading lessons in the first-floor hallway, brought to us by—you guessed it—the junior varsity cheerleaders.

I couldn't find Kenny anywhere, but I ran into Lilly at the Students for Amnesty International booth (Students Against the Corporatization of Albert Einstein High School did not submit their application for a booth in time to get one, so Lilly is stuck running the Amnesty International booth instead). And guess what? Guess who got an F in something?

That's right.

Lilly. I couldn't believe it.

"Mrs. Spears gave you an F in English? *YOU* got an F?"

She didn't seem too bothered by it, though.

"I had to take a stand, Mia," she said. "And sometimes, when you believe in something, you have to make sacrifices."

"Sure," I said. "But an *F*? Your parents are going to kill you."

"No, they won't," Lilly said. "They'll just try to psychoanalyze me."

Which is true.

Oh, God. Here comes Tina.

I hope she doesn't remember—

She does.

We're going over to the Computer Club's booth right now.

I don't want to go to the Computer Club's booth. I already looked over there, and I know what's going on. Michael and Judith and the rest of the computer nerds are sitting there behind all these color monitors. When somebody comes up, they get to sit down in front of one of the monitors, and play a computer game the club designed where you walk through the school and all of the teachers are in funny costumes. Like Principal Gupta is wearing a leather dominatrix's outfit, and holding a whip, and Mr. Gianini is in footie pajamas with a teddy bear that looks exactly like him.

They used a different program when the club

applied to be part of the Carnival, of course, so none of the teachers or administrators know what everyone is sitting there looking at. You would think they'd wonder why all of the kids are laughing so hard.

Whatever. I don't want to do it. I don't want to go anywhere near it.

But Tina says I have to.

"Now's the perfect time to tell him," she says. "I mean, Kenny's nowhere to be seen."

Oh, God. This is what comes from telling your friends anything.

Even later on Friday, December 19, still the Winter Carnival

Well, I'm in the girls' room again. And I think I can state with certainty that this time, I'm never coming out.

No, I think I'll just stay in here until everyone has gone home. Only then will it be safe. Thank God I am leaving the country tomorrow. Maybe by the time I get back, everyone involved in this little incident will have forgotten about it.

But I doubt it. Not with my luck, anyway.

Why do these kinds of things always happen to me? I mean, seriously? What did I ever do to turn the gods against me? Why don't these kinds of things ever happen to Lana Weinberger? Why me? Why always *me*?

All right, so here's what happened.

I had no intention whatsoever of actually telling Michael anything. I mean, let me get that out right away. I was only going along with Tina because, well, it would have looked weird if I had completely avoided the Computer Club's booth. Plus Michael had asked me so many times to make sure I stopped by. So there was no way I could avoid it.

But I never intended to say a word about You-Know-What. I mean, Tina was just going to have to learn to live with the disappointment. You don't love somebody for, like, as long as I have loved Michael and then just go up to him at a school fair and be like, "Oh, by the way, yeah, I love you."

Okay? You don't *do* that.

But whatever. So I went up to the stupid booth with Tina. Everyone was all giggly and excited, because their program was so popular that there was this really long line to see it. But Michael saw us, and went, "Come on up!"

Like we were supposed to cut in front of all these other people. I mean, we did it, of course, but everyone behind us grumbled, and who can blame them? They'd been waiting a long time.

But I guess because of the thing the night before—you know, when I explained on national television that the only reason I'd done that clothing ad was because the designer was donating all the proceeds to Greenpeace—I have been noticeably more popular (positive comments so far: 243. Negative: 1. From Lana, of course). So the grumbling wasn't as bad as it could have been.

Anyway, Michael was all, "Here, Mia, sit at this one." And he pulled out a chair in front of this one computer monitor.

So I sat down and waited for the stupid thing to come on, and all around me other kids were laughing at what they were seeing on their screens. I just sat there thinking, for some reason, *Faint heart never won fair lady*.

Which was stupid, because, number one, I was NOT going to tell him I like him and number two, Michael is dark-haired, *not* fair. And he isn't a lady either, obviously.

Then I heard Judith go, "Wait, what are you doing?"

And then I heard Michael say, "No, that's okay. I have a special one for her."

Then the screen in front of my eyes flickered. I sighed. *Okay*, I thought. *Here goes the stupid teacher thing. Be sure to laugh so they think you like it.*

So I was sitting there, and I was actually kind of depressed, because I really didn't have anything to look forward to, if you think about it. I mean, everybody else was all excited, because later on they were going to the dance, but no one had asked me to the dance—not even my supposed boyfriend—so I didn't even have that to look forward to. And everyone else I knew was going skiing or to the Bahamas or wherever for Winter Break, but what did I get to do? Oh, hang out with a bunch of members of the Genovian Olive Growers Society. I'm sure they are all really nice people, but come on.

And before I even leave for my boring trip to Genovia, I have to break up with Kenny, something I totally don't want to do, because I really do like him, and I don't want to hurt his feelings, but I guess I sort of have to.

Although I have to say, the fact that he still hasn't so much as mentioned the dance is making the idea of breaking up with him seem a lot less heinous.

Then tomorrow, I thought, *I'll leave for Europe on a plane with Dad and Grandmère, who still aren't speaking to each other* (and since I'm not speaking to Grandmère either, it should be a really fun flight), *and when I come back, knowing my luck, Michael and Judith will be engaged.*

That's what I was sitting there thinking in the split second the screen in front of me flickered. That, and, *You know, I'm not really in the mood to see any of my teachers in funny outfits.*

Only when the flickering stopped, that's not what I saw. What I saw instead was this castle.

Seriously. It was a castle, like out of the Knights of the Round Table, or *Beauty and the Beast,* or whatever. The picture zoomed in until we were over the castle walls and inside this courtyard, where there was a garden. And in the garden, all these big, fat, red roses were blooming. Some of the roses had lost their petals, and you could see them lying on the courtyard floor. It was really, really pretty, and I was like, *Hey, this is cooler than I thought it would be.*

And I sort of forgot I was sitting there in front of a computer monitor at the Winter Carnival, with like two dozen people all around me. I began to feel like I was actually *in* that garden.

Then this banner waved across the screen, in front

of the roses, like it was blowing in the wind. The banner had some words written on it in gold leaf. When it stopped flapping, I could read what the words said:

Roses are red
Violets are blue
You may not know it
But I love you, too

I screamed and jumped up out of my chair, tipping it over behind me.

Everyone started laughing. I guess they thought I'd seen Principal Gupta in her leather catsuit.

Only Michael knew I hadn't.

And Michael wasn't laughing.

Only I couldn't look at Michael. I couldn't look anywhere, really, except at my own feet. Because I couldn't believe what had just happened. I mean, I couldn't process it. What did it *mean*? Did it mean Michael knew I was the one who'd been sending him those notes, and that he felt the same way?

Or did it mean he knew I was the one who'd been sending him those notes, and he was trying to get back at me, as a kind of joke?

I didn't know. All I knew was that if I didn't get out of there, I was going to start crying . . .

. . . and in front of everyone in the entire school.

I grabbed Tina by the arm and yanked her, *hard*,

after me. I guess I was figuring I could tell her what I'd seen, and maybe *she'd* be able to figure out what it meant, since I sure couldn't.

Tina shrieked—I must have grabbed her harder than I thought—and I heard Michael call, "Mia!"

But I just kept going, lugging Tina behind me, and pushing through the crowd for the door, thinking only one thing:

Must get to the girls' room. Must get to the girls' room before I start bawling my head off.

Somebody, with about as much force as I'd grabbed Tina, grabbed me. I thought it was Michael. I knew if I so much as looked at him, I'd burst into big baby sobs. I said, "Get *off*," and jerked my arm away.

It was Kenny's voice that said, "But Mia, I *have* to talk to you!"

"Not *now*, Kenny," Tina said.

But Kenny was totally inflexible. He went, "Yes, *now*," and you could tell from his face he meant it.

Tina rolled her eyes and backed off. I stood there, my back to the Computer Club's booth, and prayed, *Please, please don't come over here, Michael. Please stay where you are. Please, please, please don't come over here.*

"Mia," Kenny said. He looked more uncomfortable than I'd ever seen him, and I've seen Kenny look plenty uncomfortable. He's an awkward kind of guy. "I just want to . . . I mean, I just want you to know. Well. That I know."

I stared at him. I had no idea what he was talking about. Seriously. I'd forgotten all about that hug he'd seen in the hallway. The one I'd given Michael. All I could think was, *Please don't come over here, Michael. Please don't come over here, Michael. . . .*

"Look, Kenny," I said. I don't even know how I got my tongue to work, I swear. I felt like a robot somebody had switched into the Off position. "This really isn't a good time. Maybe we could talk later—"

"Mia," Kenny said. He had a funny look on his face. "I *know*. I saw him."

I blinked.

And then I remembered. Michael, and the B-minus hug.

"Oh, Kenny," I said. "Really. That was just . . . I mean, there's nothing—"

"You don't have to worry," Kenny said. And then I realized why his face looked so funny. It was because he was wearing an expression on it that I had never seen before. At least, not on Kenny. The expression was resignation. "I won't tell Lilly."

Lilly! Oh, God! The last person in the world I wanted to know how I felt about Michael!

Maybe it wasn't too late. Maybe there was still a chance I could . . .

But no. No, I couldn't lie to him. For once in my life, I could not summon up a lie.

"Kenny," I said. "I am so, so sorry."

I didn't realize until I said it that it was too late to run for the girls' room: I had already started crying. My voice broke, and when I put my hands to my face, they came away wet.

Great. I was crying, and in front of the entire student body of Albert Einstein High School.

"Kenny," I said, sniffling. "I honestly meant to tell you. And I really do like you. I just don't . . . love you."

Kenny's face was very white, but he didn't start crying—not like me. Thank God. In fact, he even managed to smile a little in that weird, resigned way as he said, shaking his head, "Wow. I can't believe it. I mean, when it first hit me, I was like *no way*. Not Mia. No way would she do that to her best friend. But . . . well, I guess it explains a lot. About, um, us."

I couldn't look him in the face any longer. I felt like a worm. Worse than a worm, because worms are very environmentally helpful. I felt like . . . like . . .

Like a fruit fly.

"I guess I've suspected for a long time that there was someone else," Kenny went on. "You never . . . well, you never exactly seemed to return my ardor when we . . . you know."

I knew. Kissed. Nice of him to bring it up though, here in the gym, in front of everyone.

"I knew you just weren't saying anything because you didn't want to hurt my feelings," Kenny said. "That's the kind of girl you are. And that's why I put off asking you to the dance," Kenny admitted. "Because I figured you'd just say no. On account of you, you know, liking someone else. I mean, I know you'd never lie to me, Mia. You're the most honest person I've ever met."

HA! Was he joking? *Me?* Honest? Obviously, he did not have the slightest clue about my nostrils.

"That's how I know how much this must be tearing you up inside. I just think you'd better tell Lilly soon," Kenny said somberly. "I started to suspect, you know, at the restaurant. And if I figured it out, other people will, too. And you wouldn't want her to hear it from somebody else."

I had reached up to try to wipe some of my tears away with my sleeve, but paused with my hand only halfway there, and stared at him. "Restaurant? What restaurant?"

"You know," Kenny said, looking uncomfortable. "That day we all went to Chinatown. You and he sat next to each other. You kept laughing. . . . You looked pretty chummy."

Chinatown? But Michael hadn't gone with us that day to Chinatown. . . .

"And you know," Kenny said, "I'm not the only one who's noticed him leaving you those roses all week, either."

I blinked. I could barely see him through my tears. "W–what?"

"You know." He looked around, then dropped his voice to a whisper. "Boris. Leaving you all those roses. I mean, come on, Mia. If you two want to carry on behind Lilly's back, that's one thing, but—"

The roaring in my ears that had been there just after I'd read Michael's poem came back. BORIS. BORIS PELKOWSKI. My boyfriend just broke up with me because he thinks I am having an affair with BORIS PELKOWSKI.

BORIS PELKOWSKI, who always has food in his braces.

BORIS PELKOWSKI, who wears his sweaters tucked inside his pants.

BORIS PELKOWSKI, my best friend's boyfriend.

Oh, God. My life is so over.

I tried to tell him. You know, the truth. That Boris isn't my secret love, but my Secret Snowflake.

But Tina darted forward, grabbed me by the arm, and went, "Sorry, Kenny, Mia has to go now." Then she dragged me into the girls' room.

"I have to tell him," I kept saying, over and over, like a crazy person, as I tried to break free of her grip. "I have to tell him. I have to tell him the truth."

"No, you do not," Tina said, pushing me past the toilet stalls. "You two are broken up. Who cares why? You're through, and that's all that matters."

I blinked at my tear-stained reflection in the mirror above the sinks. I looked awful. Never in your life have you seen anyone who looked less like a princess than I did just then. Just looking at myself made me break out into a fresh new wave of tears.

Of course Tina says she's sure Michael wasn't trying to make fun of me. Of course she says that he must have figured out that I was the one who was sending him those cards and was trying to let me know that he felt the same way about me.

Only of course I can't believe that. Because if that were true—*if that were true*—why did he let me go? Why didn't he try to stop me?

Tina has pointed out that he did try. But my shrieking when I read his poem, and then running in tears from the room, might not have seemed to him like a very encouraging sign. In fact, it might have actually looked to him like I was displeased by what I'd seen. Furthermore, Tina pointed out, even if Michael had tried to go after me, there'd been Kenny cornering me on my way out. It had certainly looked as if the two of us were Having A Moment—which we most certainly were—and didn't wish to be disturbed.

All of which could be true.

But it could also be true that Michael had just been joking. It was a very mean joke, under the circumstances, but Michael doesn't know that I adore him with every fiber of my being. Michael doesn't know that I've been in love with him all my life. Michael doesn't know that without him, I will never, ever achieve self-actualization. I mean, to Michael, I'm just his kid sister's best friend. He probably didn't mean to be cruel. He probably thought he was being funny.

It isn't his fault that my life is over, and that I am never, ever leaving this bathroom.

I'll just wait until everybody is gone, and then I'll sneak out, and no one will see me again until next semester starts, by which time, hopefully, all of this will have blown over.

Or, better yet, maybe I'll just stay in Genovia. . . .

Hey, yeah. Why not?

I don't know why people can't just leave me alone.

Seriously. I may be done with finals, but I still have a lot to do. I mean, I have to pack, don't I? Don't people know that when you are leaving for your royal introduction to the people over whom you will one day reign, you have to do a lot of packing?

But no. No, people keep on calling, and e-mailing, and coming over.

Well, I'm not talking to anybody. I think I have made that perfectly clear. I am not speaking to Lilly or Tina or my dad or Mr. Gianini or my mother and ESPECIALLY not Michael, even though at last count, he'd called four times.

I am *way* too busy to talk to anybody.

And with my headphones on, I can't even hear them pounding on the door. It's kind of nice, I have to say.

People have a right to their privacy. If I want to go into my room and lock the door and not come out or have to deal with anyone, I should have a right to. People should *not* be allowed to take the hinges off of my door and *remove* it. That is completely unfair.

But I have found a way to foil them. I am out on the fire escape. It's about thirty degrees out here, and snowing, by the way, but guess what? So far no one has followed me.

Fortunately I bought one of those pens that's also a flashlight, so I can see to write. The sun went down a while ago, and I have to admit, my butt is freezing. But it's actually sort of nice out here. All you can hear is the hiss of the snow as it lands on the metal of the fire escape, and the occasional siren or car alarm. It is restful, in a way.

And you know what I'm finding out? I need a rest. Big time.

Really. I need to like, go and lie on a beach somewhere, or something.

There's a nice beach in Genovia. Really. With white sand, palm trees, the whole bit.

Too bad while I'm there, I'm never going to have time to visit it, since I'm going to be too busy christening battleships, or whatever.

But if I *lived* in Genovia . . . you know, moved there,

and lived there full time . . .

Oh, I'll miss my mom, of course. I've already considered that. She's leaned out the window about twenty times already, begging me to come inside or at least put on a coat. My mom's a nice lady. I'll really miss her.

But she can come visit me in Genovia. At least up until her eighth month. Then air travel might be a little risky. But she can come after my baby brother or sister is born. That would be nice.

And Mr. G, he's okay, too. He just leaned out and asked if I wanted any of the four-alarm chili he just made. He left out the meat, he says, just for me.

That was nice of him. He can come visit me in Genovia, too.

It will be nice to live there. I can hang out with my dad all the time. He's not such a bad guy, either, once you get to know him. He wants me to come in off the fire escape, too. I guess my mom must have called him. He says he's really proud of me, on account of the press conference and my B minus in Algebra and all. He wants to take me out to dinner to celebrate. We can go to the Zen Palate, he says. A totally vegetarian restaurant. Isn't that nice of him?

Too bad he let Lars take my door down, or I might have gone with him.

Ronnie, our next door neighbor, just looked out her window and saw me. Now she wants to know what I'm doing, sitting out on the fire escape in December.

I told her I needed some privacy, and that this appears to be the only way I can get it.

Ronnie went, "Honey, don't I know how that is."

She said I was going to freeze without a coat though, and offered me her mink. I politely declined, as I cannot wear the skins of dead animals.

So she loaned me her electric blanket, which she has plugged into the outlet beneath her air conditioner. I must say, this is an improvement.

Ronnie's getting ready to go out. It's nice to watch her put on her makeup. As she does it, she keeps up a running conversation with me through her open window. She asked me if I was having trouble at school, and if that was why I'm on the fire escape, and I said I was. She asked what kind, and I told her. I told her I am being persecuted: that I am in love with my best friend's brother, but that to him it is apparently all this really big joke. Oh, and also that everyone apparently thinks I am having an affair with a mouth-breathing violinist who happens to be my best friend's boyfriend.

Ronnie shook her head and said it was good to know things haven't changed since she was in high school. She says she knows what it is like to be persecuted, because Ronnie used to be a man.

I told Ronnie that it really doesn't matter, because I'm moving to Genovia. Ronnie said she was sorry to hear that. She'll miss me, as I have really improved conditions in the apartment building's incinerator room since I insisted on installing separate recycling bins for newspapers and cans and bottles.

Then Ronnie said she has to go because she's meeting her boyfriend for cocktails at the Carlyle. She said I could keep using the electric blanket, though, so long as I remember to return it when I'm done.

God. Even my next door neighbor, who used to be a man, has a boyfriend. WHAT IS WRONG WITH ME????

Uh-oh. I hear footsteps in my room. Who's coming now?

Well. You could knock me over with a feather.

Guess who just came out onto the fire escape and sat with me for half an hour?

Grandmère.

I'm not even kidding.

I was sitting here, feeling all depressed, when all of a sudden this big furry sleeve appeared out my window, and then a foot in a high-heeled shoe, and then a big blond head, and next thing I knew, Grandmère was sitting there, blinking at me from the depths of her full-length chinchilla.

"Amelia," she said, in her most no-nonsense tone. "What are you doing out here? It's snowing. Come back inside."

I was shocked. Shocked that Grandmère would even consider coming out onto the fire escape (it's an indelicate thing for a princess to mention, but there is actually a lot of bird poop out here), but also that she would dare to speak to me, after what she did.

But she addressed that issue right away.

"I understand that you are upset with me," she said. "And you have a right to be. But I want you to know that what I did, I did for you."

"Oh, right!" Even though I swore I was never going to speak to her again, I couldn't help myself. "Grandmère, how can you possibly say that? You completely humiliated me!"

"I didn't mean to," Grandmère said. "I meant to show you that you are just as pretty as those girls in the magazines you are always wishing you look like. It's important that you know that you are not this hideous creature that you apparently think you are."

"Grandmère," I said. "That's nice of you and all— I guess—but you shouldn't have done it that way."

"What other way could I do it?" Grandmère demanded. "You will not pose for any of the magazines that have offered to send photographers. Not for *Vogue*, or *Harper's Bazaar*. Don't you understand that what Sebastiano said about your bone structure is really true? You really are quite beautiful, Amelia. If only you'd just have a little more confidence in yourself, show off once in a while. Think how quickly that boy you like would leave the housefly girl for you!"

"Fruit fly," I said. "And Grandmère, I told you, Michael likes her because she's really smart. They have a lot of stuff in common, like computers. It has nothing to do with how she looks."

"Oh, Mia," Grandmère said. "Don't be naive."

Poor Grandmère. It really wasn't fair to blame her, because she comes from such a different world. In Grandmère's world, women are valued for being great beauties—or, if they aren't great beauties, they are revered for dressing impeccably. What they do, like for a living, isn't important, because most of them don't do anything. Oh, maybe they do some charity work, or whatever, but that's it.

Grandmère doesn't understand, of course, that today being a great beauty doesn't count for much. Oh, it matters in Hollywood, of course, and on the runways in Milan. But nowadays, people understand that perfect looks are the result of DNA, something the person has nothing to do with. It's not like it's any great accomplishment, being beautiful. That's just genetics.

No, what matters today is what you do with the brain *behind* those perfect blue eyes, or brown eyes, or green, or whatever. In Grandmère's day, a girl like Judith, who could clone fruit flies, would be viewed as a piteous freak, unless she managed to clone fruit flies *and* look stunning in Dior.

And even in this remarkably enlightened age, girls like Judith still don't get as much attention as girls like Lana—which isn't fair, since cloning fruit flies is probably way more important than having totally perfect hair.

The really pathetic people are the ones like me: I can't clone fruit flies, *and* I've got bad hair.

But that's okay. I'm used to it by now.

Grandmère's the one who still needs convincing that I am an absolutely hopeless case.

"Look," I said to Grandmère. "I told you. Michael is not the type of guy who is going to be impressed because I'm in a *Sunday Times* supplement in a strapless ballgown. *That's why I like him.* If he were the kind of guy who was impressed by stuff like that, I wouldn't want anything to do with him."

Grandmère didn't look very convinced.

"Well," she said. "Perhaps you and I must agree to disagree. In any case, Amelia, I came over to apologize. I never meant to distress you. I meant only to show you what you can do, if you'd only try." She spread her gloved hands apart. "And look how well I succeeded. Why, you planned and executed an entire press conference, all on your own!"

I couldn't help smiling a little at that one. "Yes," I said. "I did."

"And," Grandmère said, "I understand that you passed Algebra."

I grinned wider. "Yes. I did."

"Now," Grandmère said, "there is only one thing left for you to do."

I nodded. "I know. I've been thinking a lot about it, and I think it might be best if I extended my stay in Genovia. Like maybe I could just live there from now on. What do you think about that?"

Grandmère's expression, I could see in the light coming from my room, was one of disbelief.

"Live in . . . live in Genovia?" For once, I'd caught her off guard. "What are you talking about?"

"You know," I said. "They have schools there. I

could just finish ninth grade there. And then maybe I could go to one of those Swiss boarding schools you're always going on about."

Grandmère just stared at me. "You'd hate it."

"No," I said. "It might be fun. No boys, right? That would be great. I mean, I'm kind of sick of boys right now."

Grandmère shook her head. "But your friends . . . your mother . . ."

"Well," I said, reasonably. "They could come visit."

Then Grandmère's face hardened. She peered at me from between the heavily mascaraed slits her eyes had become.

"Amelia Mignonette Grimaldi Renaldo," she said. "You are running away from something, aren't you?"

I shook my head innocently. "Oh, no, Grandmère," I said. "Really. I'd like to live in Genovia. It'd be neat."

"NEAT?" Grandmère stood up. Her high heels went through the slots between the metal bars of the fire escape, but she didn't notice. She pointed imperiously at my window.

"You get inside right now," she ordered, in a voice I had never heard her use before.

I have to admit, I was so startled, I did exactly what she said. I unplugged Ronnie's electric blanket and crawled right back into my room. Then I stood there while Grandmère crawled back in, too.

"You," she said, when she'd straightened out her

skirt, "are a princess of the royal house of Renaldo. A princess," she said, going to my closet, and rifling through it, "does not shirk her responsibilities. Nor does she run at the first sign of adversity."

"Um, Grandmère," I said. "What happened today was hardly the first sign of adversity, okay? What happened today was the last straw. I can't take it anymore, Grandmère. I'm getting out."

Grandmère pulled from my closet the dress Sebastiano had designed for me to wear to the dance. You know, the one that was supposed to make Michael forget that I am his little sister's best friend.

"Nonsense," Grandmère said.

That was all.

Just nonsense. Then she stood there, tapping her toes, staring at me.

"Grandmère," I said. Maybe it was all that time I'd spent outside. Or maybe it was that I was pretty sure my mom and Mr. G and my dad were all in the next room, listening. How could they not be? There was no *door*, or anything, to separate my room from the living room.

"You don't understand," I said. "I can't go back there."

"All the more reason," Grandmère said, "for you to go."

"No," I said. "First of all, I don't even have a date

for the dance, okay? And P.S., only losers go to dances without dates."

"You are not a loser, Amelia," Grandmère said. "You are a princess. And princesses do not run away when things become difficult. They throw their shoulders back, and they face what disaster awaits them head on. Bravely, and without complaint."

I said, "Hello, we are not talking about marauding visigoths, okay, Grandmère? We are talking about an entire high school that seems to think that I am in love with Boris Pelkowski."

"Which is precisely," Grandmère said, "why you must show them that it doesn't matter to you what they think."

"Why can't I show them that it doesn't matter by not going?"

"Because that," Grandmère said, "is the cowardly way. And you, Mia, as you have shown amply this past week, are not a coward. Now get dressed."

I don't know why I did what she said. Maybe it was because somewhere deep inside, I knew that for once, Grandmère was right.

Or maybe it was because secretly, I guess I was a little curious to see what would happen.

But I think the real reason was because, for the first time in my entire life, Grandmère didn't call me Amelia.

No. She called me Mia.

And because of my stupid sentimentalism, I am in a car right now, going back to stupid, crappy Albert Einstein High School, the dust from which I thought I'd managed to shake permanently from my feet not four hours ago.

But no. Oh, no. I'm going back, in the stupid velvet party dress Sebastiano designed for me. I'm going back, with no date. I'm going back, and I will probably be ridiculed for being the dateless biological freak that I am.

I am, however, a princess, and apparently that means I am expected to take whatever is dished out at me, no matter how cruel, unfair, or undeserved it might be.

And regardless of what happens, I can always comfort myself with the knowledge of one thing:

Tomorrow, I will be thousands of miles away from all of this.

Oh, God. We're here.

I think I'm going to be sick.

When I was about to turn six years old, all I wanted for my birthday was a cat.

I didn't care what kind of cat. I just wanted one. I wanted a cat of my very own. We had been to visit my mom's parents at their farm in Indiana, and they had a lot of cats. One of them had had kittens, little fluffy orange and white ones, which purred loudly when I held them under my chin, and liked to curl up inside the bib of my overalls and take naps. More than anything in the world, I wanted to keep one of those kittens.

I should mention that at the time, I had a thumb-sucking problem. My mother had tried everything to get me to stop sucking my thumb, including buying me a Barbie, in spite of her fundamental stand against Barbie and all that she stands for, as a sort of bribe. Nothing worked.

So when I started whining to her about wanting a kitten, my mom came up with a plan. She told me she would get me a kitten for my birthday if I quit sucking my thumb.

Which I did, immediately. I wanted a cat of my own *that badly.*

Yet, as my birthday rolled around, I had my doubts my mother would live up to her end of the bargain. For one thing, even at the age of six, I knew my mom wasn't the most responsible person. Why else was our electricity always being turned off? And about half the time I would show up at school wearing a skirt AND pants, because my mother let *me* decide what to wear. So I wasn't sure she'd remember about the kitten—or that, if she did remember, she'd know where to get one.

So as you can imagine, when the morning of my sixth birthday rolled around, I wasn't holding out much hope.

But when my mother came into my bedroom holding this tiny ball of yellow and white fur, and plopped it onto my chest, and I looked into Louie's (he didn't become Fat Louie until about twenty-something pounds later) great big blue eyes (this was before they turned green), I knew a joy such as I had never known before in my life, and never expected to feel again.

That is, until last night.

I am totally serious.

Last night was the best night of my ENTIRE life. After that whole fiasco with Sebastiano and the photos, I thought I would never ever feel anything like gratitude to Grandmère EVER again.

But she was SO RIGHT to make me go to that dance. I am SO GLAD I went back to Albert Einstein, the best, the loveliest school in the whole country, if not the whole world!!!!!!!

Okay, here's what happened:

Lars and I pulled up in front of the school. There were twinkly white lights in all the windows, that I guess were supposed to represent icicles, or whatever.

I was sure I was going to throw up and I mentioned this to Lars. He said I couldn't possibly throw up because to his certain knowledge I hadn't eaten anything since the Entenmann's cake way before lunch, and that was probably all digested by now. With that piece of encouraging information, he escorted me up the steps and into the school.

There were masses of people teeming around the coat check in the front entrance. Lars checked our coats while I stood there waiting for someone to come up and ask me what I was doing there without a date. All that happened, however, was that Lilly-and-Boris and Tina-and-Dave descended upon me and started acting all nice and said how happy they were that I'd come (Tina told me later that she'd already explained to everyone that Kenny and I had broken up, although she hadn't told them why, THANK GOD).

So, fortified, by my friends, I went into the gym, which was decorated all wintry, with cut-out paper snowflakes, one of those disco balls, and fake snow everywhere, which I must say looked a lot whiter and cleaner than the snow that was starting to pile up on the ground outside.

There were tons of people there. I saw Lana and Josh (ugh), Justin Baxendale with his usual flock of adoring fans, and Shameeka and Ling Su and a bunch of other people. Even Kenny was there, though when he saw me, he turned bright red and turned around and started talking to this girl from our Bio class. Oh well.

Everyone was there, except the one person I'd been most dreading. Or hoping to see. I didn't know which.

Then I saw Judith Gershner. She had changed out of her overalls and looked quite pretty in this red Laura Ashley-ish dress.

But she wasn't dancing with Michael. She was dancing with some boy I'd never seen before.

So I looked around for Lilly, and finally spotted her using one of the pay phones. I went up to her and was like, "Where's your brother?"

Lilly hung up the phone. "How should I know?" she demanded. "It's not my turn to baby-sit him."

Oddly comforted by her demeanor—which simply proved that no matter how much other things change, Lilly always stayed the same—I went, "Well, Judith Gershner is here, so I just figured—"

"For God's sake," Lilly said. "How many times do I have to tell you? *Michael and Judith are not going out.*"

I went, "Oh, right. Then why have they spent every waking moment together for the past two weeks?"

"Because they were working on that stupid computer program for the Carnival," she said. "Besides, Judith Gershner already has a boyfriend." Lilly grabbed me by the shoulders and turned me around so I could see Judith on the dance floor. "He goes to Trinity."

I looked at Judith Gershner as she slow-danced with

a boy who looked a lot like Kenny, only older and not as uncoordinated.

"Oh," I said.

"*Oh* is right," Lilly said. "I don't know what is wrong with you today, but I can't deal with you when you're acting like such a freak. Sit down right here—" She pulled out a chair. "And don't you dare get up. I want to know where to find you when I need to."

I didn't even ask Lilly why she might need to find me. I just sat down. I felt like I couldn't stand up anymore. I was *that* tired.

It wasn't that I was disappointed. I mean, I didn't want to see Michael. At least, part of me didn't.

Another part of me *really* wanted to see him and ask him just what he'd meant by that poem.

But I was sort of afraid of the answer.

Because it might not be the one I was hoping it would be.

After a while, Lars and Wahim came and sat down next to me. I felt like a complete tool. I mean, there I was, sitting at a dance with two bodyguards, who were deep in a discussion about the advantages versus the disadvantages of rubber bullets. Nobody was asking me to dance. Nobody would, either. I mean, I'm a huge, colossal loser. A huge, colossal loser without a date.

Who, by the way, is supposedly in love with Boris Pelkowski.

Why was I even staying? I had done what

Grandmère said. I had shown up. I had proved to everyone that I wasn't a coward. Why couldn't I leave? I mean, if I wanted to?

I stood up. I said to Lars, "Come on. We've been here long enough. I still have a lot of packing to do. Let's go."

Lars said okay, and started to get up. Then he stopped. I saw that he was looking at something behind me. I turned around.

And there was Michael.

He had obviously just gotten there. He was out of breath. His bow tie wasn't tied. And there was still snow in his hair.

"I didn't think you were coming," he said.

I knew my face had gone as red as Judith Gershner's dress. But there wasn't anything I could do about that. I said, "Well, I almost didn't."

He said, "I called you a bunch of times. Only you wouldn't come to the phone."

I said, "I know." I was wishing the floor of the gym would open up, like in *It's a Wonderful Life*, and that I'd fall into the pool underneath it and drown and not have to have this conversation.

"Mia," he said. "With that thing today. I didn't mean to make you cry."

Or the floor would open and I could just fall, and keep falling, forever and ever and ever. That would be okay, too. I stared at the floor, willing it to crack apart and swallow me up.

"It didn't." I lied. "I mean, it wasn't that. It was something Kenny said."

"Yeah," Michael said. "Well, I heard you two broke up."

Yeah. Probably by now the whole school had. Now, I knew, my face was even redder than Judith's dress.

"The thing is," Michael went on, "I knew it was you. Who was leaving those cards."

If he had reached inside my chest, pulled out my heart, flung it to the floor, and kicked it across the room, it could not possibly have hurt as much as hearing that. I could feel my eyes filling up with tears all over again.

"You did?" You know, it's one thing to have your heart broken. But to have it happen at a school dance, in front of everyone . . . well, that's harsh.

"Of course I did," he said. He sounded impatient. "Lilly told me."

For the first time, I looked up into his face.

"*Lilly* told you?" I cried. "How did *she* know?"

He waved his hand. "I don't know. Your friend Tina told her, I guess. But that's not important."

I looked around the gym and saw Lilly and Tina on the far side of it, both staring in my direction. When they saw me looking at them, they turned around really fast and pretended to be deeply absorbed in conversation with their dates.

"I'm going to kill them," I murmured.

Michael reached out and grabbed both my shoulders. "Mia," he said, giving me a little shake. "It doesn't *matter*. What matters is that I meant what I wrote. And I thought you did, too."

I didn't think I could have heard him right. I went, "Of course I meant it."

He shook his head. "Then why did you freak out like that today at the Carnival?"

I stammered, "Well, because . . . because . . . I thought . . . I thought you were making fun of me."

"Never," he said.

And that's when he did it.

No fuss. No asking my permission. No hesitation whatsoever. He just leaned down and kissed me, right on the lips.

And I found out, right then, that Tina was right:

It *isn't* gross if you're in love with the guy.

In fact, it's the nicest thing in the whole world.

And do you know what the best part is?

I mean, aside from Michael being in love with me, and having kept it a secret almost as long as I have, if not longer?

And Lilly knowing all along but not saying anything up until a few days ago because she found it an interesting social experiment to see how long it would take us to figure it out on our own (a long time, it turned out)?

And the fact that Michael's going to Columbia next year, which is only a few subway stops away, so I'll still be able to see him as much as I want?

Oh, and Lana walking by while we were kissing, and going, in this disgusted voice, "Oh, God, get a room, would you please?"

And slow dancing with him all night long, until Lilly finally came up and said, "Come on you guys, it's snowing so hard, if we don't leave now, we'll never get home"?

And kissing good night outside the stoop to my loft, with the snow falling all around us (and grumpy Lars complaining he was getting cold)?

No, the best part is that we moved right into Frenching without any trouble at all. Tina was right— it just seemed perfectly natural.

And now the royal Genovian flight attendant says we have to put away our tray tables for takeoff, so I'll have to quit writing in a minute.

Dad says if I don't stop talking about Michael, he's going to go sit up front with the pilot for the flight.

Grandmère says she can't get over the change in me. She says I seem taller. And you know, maybe I am. She thinks it's because I'm wearing another one of Sebastiano's original creations, designed just for me, just like the dress that was supposed to make Michael see me as more than just his little sister's best friend . . .

except that it turned out he did anyway. But I know that's not it.

And it isn't love, either. Well, not entirely.

I'll tell you what it is: self-actualization.

Well, that and the fact that it turns out I'm really a princess, after all. I must be, because guess what?

I'm living happily ever after.

And the best part is,
there are many more books by
Meg Cabot!

Turn the page for excerpts from:

- Mia lives happily ever after in *The Princess Diaries, Volume IV: Princess in Waiting* . . . or does she?

- #1 *New York Times* best-seller *All-American Girl* tells the story of Samantha Madison, national heroine—and maybe the object of the First Son's affections.

- Plus the whole list of Meg Cabot's royally fabulous books!

From

The Princess Diaries, Volume IV:

Princess in Waiting

Saturday, January 3
Royal Daily Schedule

8 a.m.–9 a.m.
Breakfast with Genovian Olympic Equestrian Team

I really have nothing against horsey people, because horses are totally cool. But *what* does the palace kitchen staff have against ketchup? Seriously, ever since I gave up on the no dairy/egg thing, on account of I can't live without cheese and McDonald's has started treating the hens that lay the eggs for their Egg McMuffins humanely, I like nothing better than an egg-and-cheese omelet for breakfast. BUT HOW CAN I ENJOY IT WITHOUT KETCHUP???? When I come back to Genovia next time, I am fully bringing a bottle of Heinz with me.

9:30 a.m.–Noon
Dedicate new modern wing of Royal Genovian Museum of Art

Hello, I paint better than some of these dudes, and

I am completely talentless. At least they put one of my mom's paintings in there (Portrait of the Artist's Daughter at Age Five Refusing to Eat Hot Dogs) so that's okay.

12:30 p.m.–2 p.m.
Lunch with Genovian ambassador to Japan
    Domo arigato.

2:30 p.m.–4:30 p.m.
Sit in on meeting of Genovian Parliament
    Again???? Spent entire session thinking about Michael. When Michael smiles, sometimes one corner of his mouth goes up higher than the other. Also, he has extremely nice lips. And very nice, dark eyes. Eyes that can see to the depths of my soul. I miss him so much!!!!!! This sucks. I should call Amnesty International—IT IS CRUEL AND UNUSUAL PUNISHMENT TO KEEP ME FROM THE MAN I LOVE FOR SO LONG!!!

5 p.m.–6 p.m.
Tea with Genovian Historical Society
    They actually had a lot of very interesting things to say about some of my relatives. It was too bad Prince René was in Monte Carlo buying a new polo pony. He might have learned a thing or two.

Formal dinner with members of Genovian Trade Association
Okay, René was lucky to miss this.

14 Days Since Last Saw Michael.
I don't think I'll be able to stand this much longer.

Poem for M. M.

Across the deep blue shining sea,
is Michael, far away from me.
But he doesn't seem so far away—
though I haven't seen him for fourteen days—
because in my heart Michael stays
and there he'll beat forever always.

I can see I am going to have to work harder if I am
to come up with a fitting tribute to my love.

Sunday, January 4
Royal Daily Schedule

9 a.m.–10 a.m.
Mass in Royal Genovian Chapel
I thought going to church was supposed to fill you
with a sense of spiritual well-being and succor. But all
I feel is sleepy.

10:30 a.m.–4 p.m.
Outing with Monaco's Royal Family, Royal Genovian Yacht

Why am I the least-tan person in Genovia? And what is up with René and the Speedos? I mean, you can totally tell he thinks he's all that. And all those girls screaming his name on the dock just encourage him. I wonder if they'd still be so crazy about him if someone told them that I caught René singing an Enrique Iglesias song in front of the mirrored wall in the Reception Room, using my scepter as a pretend microphone?

4:30 p.m.–7 p.m.
Princess lessons with Grandmère

Even in Genovia, it doesn't end. As if I don't totally get why everybody is so mad about the whole speech thing. I mean, I have already sworn I will never again veer from the prepared script while addressing the Genovian populace. Why does she have to keep HARPING?

7 p.m.–10 p.m.
Formal dinner with prime minister of France and his family

René disappeared for four hours with the prime minister's twenty-year-old daughter. They said they just went to play roulette, but if that's true, why were they smirking so much when they got back? If René doesn't watch it, he is going to have a Little Prince to look out for, sooner than he thinks.

15 DSLSM

Tried to call him twice today. Michael's grand-mother answered the first time, and said Michael had gone to the computer store to buy a new toner cartridge. Then his dad answered and said Michael and Lilly had gone with their grandparents to go see the latest James Bond at the dollar cinema. Lucky ducks!!!!!!!!!!!!!!!!!!!!!!!

Read all of the books about Princess Mia!

The Princess Diaries

Mia learns she is a princess, receives her first kiss, and is equally befuddled by both.

The Princess Diaries, Volume II:
Princess in the Spotlight

Mia has a wedding to plan (not hers!), a visiting cousin on the loose, and best of all, a secret admirer.

The Princess Diaries, Volume III:
Princess in Love

Hello, you just read this! Wasn't it romantic?

The Princess Diaries, Volume IV:
Princess in Waiting

Mia's in love, but she's also in Genovia being presented to her people, taking more princess lessons, and trying to schedule a first date with her long-sought-after royal consort.

Mia reveals all of her secrets in

Princess Lessons

A Princess Diaries Book

Yes! Finally!
The handbook you've been waiting for!
This manual has it all:

- ← Preventing your tiara from slipping off
- ← Writing that perfect term paper
- ← Keeping your pores squeaky clean
- ← Winning the heart of the boy of your dreams (or, at the very least, the cute guy you sit next to in language lab)
- ← Avoiding a military incursion by a neighboring principality
- ←And much, much more!

By following the invaluable advice of Mia and her very special guest authors (including best friend and urban guerrilla Lilly Moscovitz; Grandmère, the dowager princess of Genovia; Manhattan beauty expert Paolo; Italian fashion specialist Sebastiano Grimaldi; and Tina Hakim Baba, resident high school romance specialist), you will be well prepared for the day you finally ascend the throne . . . or at the very least, you'll know the difference between a fish fork and a salad fork.

Be sure to read Meg Cabot's

ALL★AMERICAN *Girl*

It only took about two hours for it to get all the way around John Adams Preparatory School that I was bringing the president's son with me as my date to Kris Parks's party on Saturday night.

For some reason this was more interesting to people than the fact that I had stopped a bullet from entering the skull of our nation's leader, or that I was the country's new teen ambassador to the UN. While I could not help but be thankful that I was no longer constantly being complimented on my bravery—all the more upsetting because I truly did not believe what I had done had been all that brave—it was somewhat disconcerting that everyone was, instead, making jokes about what might or might not have gone on between the president's son and me in the Lincoln Bedroom.

"Look, you're taking this the wrong way," Lucy said when I remarked upon this at the kitchen table after school. "The fact that you and this David dude are an item—DO NOT PINCH ME AGAIN—is only going to elevate your already sky-high stock. You, Sam, are the new It Girl of Adams Prep. If you would just give up the whole black-on-black thing, you could be voted prom queen like *that*." Lucy snapped her fingers in the air, and Manet hurried over, thinking she might have dropped some of the chocolate chip cookies Theresa had made and that we were all now chowing down on.

"Well, I don't want to be prom queen," I said. "I just want things to be back to normal."

"I'm going to take a wild guess that *that*'s not going to happen real soon," Jack said. He pointed to the reporters we could see holding their cameras up over the backyard fence, hoping to snap a picture of us through the glass atrium.

"Jesu Cristo," Theresa said, and she went to the phone to call the police again.

I sunk my chin down into my hand and went, "I just don't see why you had to tell everybody that. I mean, it is so far from the truth." I said this very clearly, so that Jack would hear. I mean, I wanted to make sure he knew that, if ever he changed his mind about Lucy, I was still available.

"How was I supposed to know what the truth is?" Lucy asked primly. "You won't tell me where the two of you disappeared to last night."

I couldn't believe she would even bring any of that up in front of Jack. Although seeing as how Lucy was unaware of Jack's status as my soul mate, I guess I couldn't really blame her.

"Because it isn't any of your business!" I cried. "I mean, you don't tell me every single thing you and Jack do together."

"Ha!" Lucy stabbed a finger at me, her smile triumphant. "I *knew* it! You two *are* going out!"

"No, we aren't," I said. "I didn't say that."

"Yes, you did. You just admitted it. You said, 'You don't tell me every single thing you and Jack do together,' which must mean you and David are going out just like Jack and I are."

"No, it doesn't," I said. "It doesn't mean that at all——"

My extremely lucid argument was interrupted, however, by Theresa, who, having gotten off the phone with the police, had then gone to intercept a package that had arrived by special delivery.

"For you," she said, setting the package down in front of me. "From the White House, the man said."

We all looked down at the package.

"See," Lucy said. "It's from David. I told you that you two are going out."

"It isn't from David," I said, opening it. "And we aren't going out."

The package turned out to be a packet of information about my new role as teen ambassador.

Lucy, seeing this, turned back to her magazine, clearly disappointed. But Jack got quite excited, reading all the little pamphlets and stuff.

"Look at this," he said. "Hey. There's going to be an international art show. From My Window, it's called. The show will feature teen artists from around the world, depicting, in a variety of mediums, what they see every day from their windows."

Rebecca, who was going over her spreadsheets down at the other end of the table, went, "What about teens who don't have windows? Such as the teen aliens who are being held against their will in Area 51? I don't think they're going to be represented, are they? Is that very fair?"

As usual, everyone ignored her.

"Hey," Jack said, getting excited. Anything involving art excited Jack. "Hey, I'm going to enter this. You should, too, Sam. They're going to display each participating country's winning entry at the UN for the month of May. That's some great exposure. And it's New York. I mean, you get something displayed in New York, you've got it made."

I was reading the letter that had come along with the From My Window pamphlet.

"I can't enter," I said with some astonishment. "I'm a judge."

"A judge?" Jack was delighted to hear it. "That's great! So I'll enter, and you pick my painting, and I'll be breaking into the New York City art scene in no time."

Rebecca looked up from her spreadsheets and stared at Jack in disbelief. "Sam can't do that," she said. "That would be cheating!"

"It's not cheating," Jack said, "if my painting is the best."

"Yeah, but what if it's not?" Lucy wanted to know. She

is the worst girlfriend. I never saw anyone so unsupportive of the man she supposedly loves!

"It will be," Jack said with a shrug of his big shoulders, like that settled that.

Jack was right, of course: his painting would be best. Jack's paintings were always the best. They had been good enough to get him into every single art show he'd ever applied to. There wasn't any doubt in my mind that next fall, in spite of his bad grades, lack of extracurriculars, and poor attendance record, Jack would get into one of the top art schools in the country, Rhode Island School of Design or Parsons or even Yale. He was just that good.

And my opinion had nothing to do with the fact that I happened to be madly in love with him.

Top ten signs that Jack loves me and not my sister Lucy and just hasn't realized it yet:

10. Whenever he sees me, he asks if I've read the latest issue of *Art in America*. He never asks Lucy if she's read it, because he knows all Lucy ever reads are fashion magazines and the Star Track section of *Parade* magazine's Sunday supplement.

9. He burned that CD for me. And true, all it had on it was whale music, which is what Jack likes to listen to while he paints, but the fact that he went to the trouble is indicative of his yearning for us to make an emotional connection.

8. He paid for my double cheeseburger meal that time at the mall when I forgot my wallet.

7. He let me have all the yellow ones out of his box of Jujubes when we all went to see the Harry Potter movie (even though technically Jack is opposed to the commercialization of children's book characters; he just went because the Jackie Chan movie playing at the theater next door was sold out).

6. He said he liked my pants that one time.

5. He complains that Lucy takes too long putting on her makeup. He told me he prefers a girl who wears no makeup. Um, that would be me. Well, except for concealer. And mascara. And lip gloss. But other than that, I wear no makeup at all.

4. When I told him my theory about how all left-handers were once part of a pair of twins, he said that made sense; he is left-handed, too, and has always felt a sense of aloneness in the world. Rebecca's theory—

that we are all descended from a race of aliens who accidentally crash-landed on this planet and lost all their advanced technological knowledge in the ensuing fiery conflagration of the mother ship—did not impress him nearly as much. And Lucy's theory—that Mr. PiBB and Dr Pepper are the same drink, just with different packaging—impressed him not at all.

3. When the Drama Club needed volunteers to paint scenery for the production of *Hello Dolly!*, Jack and I both signed up, and later ended up painting *the same plywood street lamp* (he did the trim, I did the highlights). If that was not kismet, I don't know what is.

2. Jack is a Libra. I am an Aquarius. Libras and Aquarians are known for getting along. Lucy, who is a Pisces, should really be going out with a Taurus or Capricorn.

And the number-one sign that Jack loves me and just doesn't know it yet:

1. *Fight Club* is his favorite book, too. Right after *Catch-22* and *Zen and the Art of Motorcycle Maintenance*.